'So,' he said at last, in a cool voice, 'you're the nursemaid.'

Nicholas Ellis made himself comfortable in the chair. He propped the stick up within easy reach, and then half raised one dark eyebrow as he saw Cathryn looking at it.

'Are you surprised to find me mobile?' he asked. 'Did you expect me to be on crutches? Or even in a wheelchair?'

'No,' said Cathryn slowly. 'Sir Charles told me that you could walk. Actually, I'm surprised to find you using a stick. I thought you were the type of man who'd refuse to use a prop like that.'

His eyebrow rose even higher. 'We've only just met, Miss Harrison,' he mocked her gently, 'and yet you already think you know the type of man I am?'

A KISS BY CANDLELIGHT

BY

JOANNA MANSELL

MILLS & BOON LIMITED
ETON HOUSE   18–24 PARADISE ROAD
RICHMOND   SURREY   TW9 1SR

First published in Great Britain 1990
by Mills & Boon Limited

© Joanna Mansell 1990

Australian copyright 1990
Philippine copyright 1990
This edition 1990

ISBN 0 263 76679 9

Set in 10 on 12 pt Linotron Palatino
01-9005-48241
Typeset in Great Britain by Centracet, Cambridge
Made and printed in Great Britain

CHAPTER ONE

'DEAR heaven, are you totally incompetent?'

As the furious male voice echoed across the office, everyone except for Cathryn jumped nervously.

'Are you talking to me?' she asked calmly, as she turned round to face her boss.

'Of course I'm talking to you, Miss Harrison!' Sir Charles Marchant brandished a neatly typed letter at her. 'This will have to be redone. The man's name is *Hetherington* not Fetherington. I won't stand much chance of getting this commission if you can't even type his name correctly!'

'Perhaps if you dictated a little more clearly I wouldn't make that kind of mistake,' replied Cathryn, her voice still perfectly composed. 'Anyway, it's very easy to put right. Only the one letter needs to be altered.'

The entire office staff held their breath. No one got away with talking to Sir Charles Marchant like that!

Sir Charles strode towards the door, and then paused there. 'I want to see you in my office in five minutes,' he stated in a very ominous tone of voice. 'Five minutes,' he repeated, his brows drawing together in a black scowl. Then he walked out, slamming the door behind him.

Cathryn turned back to the junior typist. Before her boss had come storming in, she had been explaining to the girl how to set out the report that she was to type.

'Is everything quite clear?' she asked. 'Sir Charles needs two copies by the end of the afternoon.'

The girl didn't even seem to hear what she was saying. Instead, she gazed up at Cathryn with wide eyes.

'Are you going to get the sack?' she breathed.

'Of course not,' Cathryn said briskly. 'I'm quite indispensable.'

'But—Sir Charles seemed so angry.'

'His temper gets the better of him sometimes,' Cathryn agreed. 'But it never lasts for very long. Now, stop worrying about me and make a start on this report. You don't want Sir Charles to get angry at *you*, do you?' she asked with a faint smile.

'No!' replied the girl, a little breathlessly, and her fingers began to fly over the keys.

As Cathryn made her way back to Sir Charles's office, though, her smile disappeared and her heart began to beat just a little faster. Outwardly, she appeared as confident and composed as ever. Inside, she could definitely feel a nervous flutter.

She knocked lightly on the door, and took a deep breath as she heard Sir Charles tell her to come in. She walked inside and saw that, instead of sitting behind his large and impressive desk, he was staring out of the huge glass window that gave him a marvellous panoramic view of London.

'I'm sorry,' he said brusquely, without even turning round to look at her. 'I shouldn't have spoken to you like that. And certainly not in front of the other staff.'

Cathryn relaxed a fraction. 'It doesn't matter,' she said.

Sir Charles turned round and thumped his hand on the desk, making her jump slightly.

'Yes, it does matter! If you like, I'll apologise to you in front of everyone.'

'Don't be silly,' Cathryn said matter-of-factly. 'You know perfectly well that isn't necessary. You lost your temper, that was all.'

A rather rueful smile spread across her boss's face. 'And you never lose yours, do you, Cathryn?' he commented. 'Perhaps that's why we work so well together. You manage to keep calm even when I'm exploding all over the place.'

Although he always referred to her as 'Miss Harrison' when other members of the staff were around, he used her Christian name when they were alone together. It didn't mean anything, though. Sir Charles was in his late forties, an extremely attractive man and a widower, but he and Cathryn had a strictly working relationship.

She certainly admired her boss, particularly for his work as an architect. No plans for soulless office blocks or dreary high-tower flats ever left Sir Charles's office. Instead, he designed very individual houses and business complexes, each with the distinctive character that stamped all of his work. In Cathryn's opinion, he was head and shoulders above most of his contemporaries, and more and more people seemed to be realising that. The commissions had been rolling in lately, and clients had to be prepared for a long wait if they wanted their building to be designed by Sir Charles Marchant.

All this had meant a much increased workload for Cathryn, but she had coped with it quite easily. She didn't mind working long hours, and even putting in an occasional weekend in order to keep up to date. It meant that she didn't have much of a social life, but that didn't bother her. Working for Sir Charles was always interesting. It also gave her the opportunity to travel, since he always took her with him when he had to go on trips abroad, and she had met some fascinating and often quite influential people.

The only small drawback was Sir Charles's temper. It was fairly unpredictable, flashing out at the most unexpected of moments, and over the last three months it seemed to have intensified. Cathryn put it down to pressure of work, and didn't allow it to upset or bother her. His outbursts were always over very quickly, and she actually preferred an open show of temper to moodiness or bottled-up emotions.

Sir Charles finally moved away from the window and sat behind his desk. His fingers tapped a restless rhythm against the beautifully polished top, and he seemed extremely edgy.

'You know that I'm going to America next week, to see some clients?' he said at last.

'Of course,' Cathryn said in surprise. 'The trip's been planned for over a month.'

'I don't want to take you with me,' he said abruptly.

Cathryn sat very still. What was coming next? she wondered warily. She had thought that Sir Charles was more than satisfied with her work, but perhaps she had been reading the signs wrongly.

He saw the look on her face, and realised at once what she was thinking. 'Don't worry,' he said with a faint smile. 'I'm not about to fire you! Where the hell would I be without you? I don't even know how I'm going to get through this American trip without you there to organise things for me.'

'Then why aren't you taking me with you?'

Sir Charles didn't answer at once. Instead, he got up and began to prowl around the office again.

'Because there's something else that I want you to do for me,' he said at last. He didn't look at her, and Cathryn had the impression that he felt very ill at ease.

'What kind of thing?' she asked with a small frown, wondering what on earth this was all about.

'A—personal favour,' replied Sir Charles, with obvious reluctance.

Cathryn blinked and tried to hide her astonishment. In all the time she had worked for Sir Charles, he had never asked her to do anything that wasn't connected with work.

'What sort of favour?' she questioned him, her curiosity growing by the minute.

Sir Charles took another turn around the room, and Cathryn wished he would sit down. All this pacing round and round was making her feel distinctly nervous!

'Have you heard of Nicholas Ellis?' he said finally, in a heavy tone.

Cathryn's well-shaped brows drew together lightly. 'Is he a client?'

'Damn it, no!' Sir Charles exploded. Then he ran his fingers tensely through his dark hair. 'Sorry,' he apologised. 'I keep lashing out in all directions today. It's just that——' He paused mid-sentence, made an obvious effort to calm himself, and sat behind the desk again. 'Don't you ever watch television?' he said drily.

'Not a great deal,' admitted Cathryn. 'There never seems to be any time.' Then she gave a small frown. 'Wait a moment. That name *does* seem familiar. I've seen it—on the news,' she said, digging deep into her memory. 'He's some kind of foreign correspondent, isn't he? Sends in reports from trouble-spots all round the world?'

'That's him,' Sir Charles confirmed a little grimly.

Cathryn's frown deepened. 'I seem to remember he got injured recently. And quite badly——'

'He got blown up,' Sir Charles said bluntly. 'He'd been travelling round with a group of guerrilla fighters in northern Africa, and was just heading back to the capital to file his report when his Jeep hit a land-mine.'

Cathryn involuntarily shivered. 'How awful! But what's all this got to do with you?'

'Nicholas Ellis is my younger brother.'

For a moment, Cathryn thought she had heard him wrongly. But Sir Charles had spoken very distinctly, which meant that he must have actually said that this man was his younger brother.

She could feel her mouth gaping open slightly, and she hurriedly shut it; then she gazed at Sir Charles.

'I didn't even know that you *had* a younger brother.'

'There's a fifteen-year age gap between us,' Sir Charles said rather abruptly. 'I'm forty-nine— Nicholas is thirty-four. And—we don't get along——'

From Sir Charles's tone of voice, Cathryn guessed that that was something of an understatement.

'Why is his surname different from yours?' she asked slowly, still trying to take all of this in.

'"Ellis" was our mother's maiden name,' Sir

Charles said, after a slight pause. 'Nicholas decided to use it very early on in his career. He was fiercely independent, even then. He didn't want to be given job opportunities because there was a title attached to the name of "Marchant".'

Cathryn knew that was something that could, and did, happen. In fact, it was one reason for Sir Charles's growing success in the States. He was an outstanding architect, but there were many excellent American architects. In straight competition he might have lost out on several commissions if there hadn't been a certain kudos attached to having your house or office complex designed by someone with a title.

All the same, there was a lot that Cathryn still didn't understand. And Sir Charles had mentioned a favour. What kind of favour did he have in mind? she wondered with growing unease. And where did his brother come into all of this?

She was about to ask him outright, but at the last moment she stopped herself. Sir Charles was clearly finding this conversation difficult enough. Perhaps she had better let him get round to it in his own good time.

'Is your brother recovering from his injuries?' she asked sympathetically.

'Nicholas was in hospital for over three months,' Sir Charles replied shortly. 'He was discharged only last week.'

'Has he gone to a convalescent home? He must be in a fairly weak state, after being in hospital for all that time.'

Sir Charles's dark brows settled themselves into a deep frown. 'He's staying at my London flat.'

'But I thought you said that you didn't get on together,' said Cathryn in surprise.

'We don't. But he *is* my brother. I feel a certain sense of responsibility for him. And they would only allow him to be discharged from the hospital on the condition that there was someone to look after him.' Sir Charles paused. 'But on Monday I'm going to the States for two weeks. Which means that there won't be anyone to look after Nicholas.'

Cathryn suddenly realised where this conversation was leading. She also decided that she didn't like it one little bit.

'There must be trained nurses you can hire,' she suggested briskly. 'They're expensive, of course, but I dare say your brother can afford it.'

'Nicholas can't, but I can,' replied Sir Charles. 'In fact, I've employed three women during the last week—and none of them stayed longer than twenty-four hours.'

'Your brother's a difficult patient?'

'Nicholas is an impossible patient.'

'Perhaps you've just been unlucky in your choice of nurses. You should try and find someone who's been trained to look after problem patients.'

Sir Charles's mouth settled into a dry smile. 'I don't think there's any training in the world that would equip someone to look after Nicholas!'

But Cathryn was determined to find a solution to Sir Charles's problem. Because if she didn't, she could see how this was going to end up.

'Why not let him return to the hospital for the couple of weeks you're away? I'm sure they wouldn't refuse to take him.'

'No, they wouldn't,' Sir Charles confirmed. 'But

Nicholas loathes hospitals. The last three months have been a nightmare for him. Our father spent the last six months of his life in hospital,' he explained quietly. 'It wasn't an easy time for him, or for us. Nicholas was in his mid-teens when it happened, which is a very impressionable time. Ever since then, he's associated hospitals with lingering death. He knows it isn't a rational association to make, but he can't help it.' Sir Charles paused. Then he turned round and looked straight at Cathryn. 'You know what I'm going to ask you, don't you?'

Cathryn was very much afraid that she did.

'You can refuse, of course,' went on Sir Charles. 'I'm asking this purely as a personal favour—and I've probably got no right to ask it at all. I don't know where else to turn, though. I *must* go to the States on Monday. There are vital contracts to be signed, people I must see. But I can't leave Nicholas on his own.'

'So you want *me* to stay with him,' said Cathryn with a distinct lack of enthusiasm.

'Yes. I don't know what commitments you have outside the office,' he added. 'I know very little about your personal life. It might not be possible for you to take on something like this.'

Cathryn had no one waiting for her at her small flat, though.

'No outside commitments,' she said in a rather toneless voice. 'But I really don't know that I can do this. Surely your brother has family? Or friends? Someone who could move in with him for a few days?'

Sir Charles shrugged. 'Our parents are both dead. As for Nicholas's friends—they're more likely to be acquaintances. My brother's always been something of a loner.'

Cathryn could feel herself being edged into a corner, and she didn't like it.

'But why *me*?' she said, a trifle desperately. 'There *must* be someone else.'

'No one I can really trust,' said Sir Charles simply. 'Apart from that, I think you're the one person I know who could cope with my brother.'

'What makes you so sure of that?'

'Because you've always coped with *my* temper, and all the ups and downs in my life. And Nicholas is like me in a lot of ways, only more—extreme,' he admitted, with some reluctance.

The more that Cathryn heard about the absent Nicholas, the less she liked the idea of spending two weeks looking after him.

'What if I say that I don't want to do this?'

Sir Charles looked resigned. 'You've every right to do that, of course. And it'll mean that I'll simply have to cancel my trip to America.'

'But you can't do that! The trip's too important.'

'I don't see that I'll have any alternative.'

Cathryn looked hard at her boss. 'This is beginning to sound rather like blackmail!'

Sir Charles's eyebrows shot up. 'Blackmail? Certainly not. I'm simply stating the alternatives.'

'No wonder you're so successful,' Cathryn said, with a wry shake of her head. 'You always know how to get your own way!'

His gaze sharpened. 'Then you'll consider my request?'

'I'll consider it,' she conceded. 'But that's all,' she warned. 'At least, for now.'

'Think about it overnight,' offered Sir Charles. 'Then you can give me your answer in the morning.'

'Before I even start to think about it, I want to know a little more about your brother. Oh, nothing too personal,' Cathryn assured him, seeing the rather wary look that crept over Sir Charles's face. 'I'm not interested in digging family skeletons out of the cupboard. I just want a few practical details.'

'What sort of details?' asked Sir Charles.

'Well, for a start, perhaps you could tell me a bit more about his injuries. Have they left him an invalid? Does your brother need actual nursing?'

'Nicholas is a long way from being fully recovered, but he doesn't need nursing,' said Sir Charles, much to Cathryn's relief. 'When the Jeep hit the land-mine, Nicholas was thrown clear—that probably saved his life. He fell awkwardly, though, and with some impact. He badly broke one leg, cracked several ribs, had some minor internal injuries, and smashed his head against a large rock, which left him with severe concussion.'

Cathryn winced and, for the first time, felt a twinge of sympathy for Sir Charles's brother.

'The ribs and internal injuries are more or less mended,' went on Sir Charles, 'and the concussion's cleared up. His leg's out of plaster, but it's still giving him quite a lot of trouble. And there's the problem of delayed shock.'

'Delayed shock?' echoed Cathryn warily.

Sir Charles gave a faint sigh. 'Nicholas is still sleeping very badly, and has vivid nightmares. He's taking medication, which should help, but it can also make him rather forgetful and lose all sense of time. Unless someone's there to make sure he takes the right pill at the right time, there's a chance he could accidentally overdose.'

Cathryn was liking the sound of this less and less. She was a personal secretary, not a nursemaid!

'I want you to know precisely what you'd be taking on,' added Sir Charles, 'so I'd better warn you that the combination of the accident and the long stay in hospital have more or less shot his nerves to pieces. He flies off the handle at the slightest provocation, and doesn't seem to care how rude or obnoxious he is. If you *do* agree to stay with him for the next couple of weeks, you certainly won't get any thanks for it from Nicholas. But you would have my extreme gratitude,' he finished quietly.

Cathryn wished that she could just say straight out that she didn't want to do this. Because she *didn't*. As far as she was concerned, Sir Charles's brother sounded thoroughly unpleasant, and she had absolutely no desire even to meet him, let alone spend the next two weeks with him.

On the other hand, this was the first time that Sir Charles had ever asked her for any sort of personal favour. And she knew how very important it was for him to go on this trip to the States.

'Look,' she said slowly, at last, 'I'll think about it. And I'll give you a decision in the morning. Is that all right?'

Sir Charles was already looking relieved that she hadn't refused him outright. 'That's fine. Now, shall we get on with some work, and forget about my damned brother until tomorrow?'

But Cathryn didn't find it that easy to put the problem of Nicholas Ellis out of her mind. It kept coming back to distract her all through the day, and then kept her awake for much of the night. The problem was, of course, that she very much wanted to refuse Sir Charles's request. It was extremely *unreasonable* of him to ask her to do something like this, she told herself crossly. But the very fact that it was so unreasonable told her just how desperate he was.

By the morning, though, she had decided that she wouldn't do it. She really didn't think she was cut out to be a nursemaid, even a temporary one. As she walked into Sir Charles's office, she was determined to tell him that. He would just have to try and find a private nurse who was made of stronger stuff than the three that Nicholas Ellis had already managed to drive out!

Then she looked at Sir Charles's anxious face, saw the faint lines of sleeplessness and worry under his eyes, and found herself telling him that she would stay with his brother for the next two weeks.

She had no idea what had made her change her mind at the last moment, and she regretted it as soon as she had said the actual words. It was too late to retract them, though. Relief had already begun to spread over Sir Charles's features, and he started to look more like his old, vital self.

'Get a taxi to my London flat on Monday morning,' he told her. 'This is the address.' He scribbled it down on a sheet of paper, and handed it to her. 'I'll introduce you to Nicholas and show you around. Then I'll head straight for the airport, to catch my flight to the States.'

Cathryn spent the whole of the weekend trying to think of some plausible excuse for not turning up at Sir Charles's flat on Monday morning. She couldn't come up with any, though, and, short of bluntly telling him that she had changed her mind, she knew she was going to have to arrive on his doorstep at nine o'clock.

She got out of bed on Monday in a thoroughly bad temper, had a quick bath, and then began to sling clothes into a suitcase. The taxi she had ordered turned up at a quarter to nine and, with a heavy sigh of reluctance, she picked up her case and set off.

Sir Charles's London flat was in a very fashionable—and expensive—part of the city. Cathryn's eyebrows lifted gently as the taxi drew up outside a large and elegant Georgian house, set in a quiet square that was surrounded by similarly impressive residences.

'*Very* nice,' she murmured under her breath. As the taxi drew away, she stood and looked at the house for a few moments. A couple of weeks of living here in quiet luxury would have been very pleasant— if it hadn't been for the fact that she was going to have to share the flat with Sir Charles's brother!

She walked up the steps and rang the bell. She could see from the name-plates that Sir Charles's flat occupied the entire ground floor of the house, and she could only guess what it cost to rent a place like this. Nor was this Sir Charles's main home. He had a large country house, where he spent any free weekends.

Cathryn was just wondering what it would be like to be able to afford this sort of lifestyle when the door opened and Sir Charles beamed down at her.

'Good. You're on time. Come in and I'll show you around.' He took her case and set it down in the hall, which was high-ceilinged, and had arched doorways leading off on either side. Sir Charles glanced at his watch. 'I don't have long, I've got to leave for the airport in fifteen minutes. I'll just show you where everything is, and then you can take it from there.'

'Fifteen minutes?' echoed Cathryn in alarm. That didn't seem much time to introduce her to his brother.

Sir Charles was already setting off on a hurried tour of the flat, though, with Cathryn scurrying along behind.

'Drawing-room, dining-room, bathroom, kitchen,' he reeled off, opening doors and offering Cathryn little more than a glimpse of each room before moving on to the next. 'Don't worry about food,' he added. 'The freezer and cupboards are stocked up with more than enough stuff to last you for two weeks. If you do want anything else, I've left the number of the local shop next to the telephone. Just ring up and tell them what you want. They'll deliver it, and put it on my account.'

Cathryn wondered what he considered to be his local shop. Harrods?

Sir Charles was already moving on, though. 'Front bedroom, guest bedroom—this is the one you'll be using, I think you'll find it quite comfortable—second bathroom, and that's Nicholas's room.'

Cathryn stared with some apprehension at the closed door which confronted them.

'Er—is your brother in there?' she asked. 'Shouldn't I meet him before you go?'

'Nicholas is still asleep,' Sir Charles said briefly. 'He's had a bad night. I thought it would be best to let him go on resting, and then you can introduce yourself when he wakes up.'

'But—you'll be gone by then,' said Cathryn, beginning to feel just a little panic-stricken. She would have much preferred to have met Nicholas for the first time while Sir Charles was still there.

But Sir Charles was already heading towards the front door, where his suitcases were waiting. 'One of the things you'll soon learn is that it's always best to let Nicholas sleep for as long as possible,' he told her in a dry voice. 'It's one of the few times when you'll get some peace and quiet.'

An impatient hoot from outside announced that his taxi had arrived.

Sir Charles turned back to Cathryn for a few moments. 'As you know, I'll be travelling around once I reach the States, but I've left a list of telephone numbers. If anything really urgent comes up, you should be able to reach me on one of those numbers, or get in touch with someone who can pass a message on to me.' He paused for a moment, and the worried look was back in his eyes again. 'You will be able to cope, won't you, Cathryn? I realise I should never have asked you to do this, but I really couldn't think of anyone else who is as capable as you are.'

Cathryn realised that he was paying her a great compliment and she flushed slightly. Sir Charles was always very sparing with his praise.

'Yes, I'll cope,' she assured him, hoping that she wasn't being over-optimistic. The taxi hooted again. 'You'd better go,' she said. 'You don't want to miss your flight.'

But Sir Charles paused in the doorway. 'Promise me that you'll stay with my brother for the whole two weeks?' he said quietly. 'You won't walk out on him, no matter what he says or does?'

'Yes, I promise,' said Cathryn, after a moment's hesitation.

He nodded in satisfaction. 'That's good enough for me. I know you're a girl who won't break your word.'

Cathryn looked up at him. 'You really do care for your brother, don't you?' she said softly.

'My feelings towards my brother are very mixed,' replied Sir Charles, the grim note back in his voice again. 'But I wouldn't walk out and leave anyone on their own in this sort of situation—not even Nicholas.' As the taxi hooted for the third time, he picked up his cases. 'See you in two weeks, Cathryn. And good luck.'

A couple of minutes later he had gone, and Cathryn was alone in the flat. No, not alone, she reminded herself, looking uneasily at the closed door. Nicholas Ellis was behind that door. And sooner or later she was going to have to meet Sir Charles's brother.

Because just the thought of it made her feel uncharacteristically nervous, she occupied herself by taking her suitcase into the guest bedroom and putting her clothes into the spacious cupboards and drawers. Then she went to the kitchen and made herself a cup of coffee.

She wished it weren't so quiet. Somehow, she found the silence rather unnerving. Her own flat was on a busy road. Although she often cursed the traffic that streamed by endlessly, she found herself missing the familiar sound of cars whizzing past, and the chatter of voices or the sound of a television programme echoing through the thin walls.

Probably the only sounds around here came from

the birds singing quietly in the trees in the square, or the soft purr of a Rolls-Royce drawing up outside one of the elegant houses!

Cathryn wondered what she was supposed to do with herself all day. Or would Nicholas Ellis prove so demanding that filling the next two weeks wouldn't be any problem?

Every time Sir Charles's brother crossed her thoughts, her nerves gave a sharp twitch. She wished she had had a chance to meet him while Sir Charles was still here. It would have made that first encounter so much easier.

She finished her coffee, and wondered whether to take a stroll around the garden. Although it was late autumn, the weather was unseasonably mild, with warm, hazy sunshine.

Anything was better than just sitting around, feeling more and more nervous, Cathryn told herself. She got to her feet, went to move towards the sink to wash up her cup, and then stopped dead as she saw the man standing motionless in the doorway, watching her.

The flat was completely silent, and yet Cathryn hadn't heard him approach. Her gaze slid to his face, and locked on to his eyes. They were green—somehow, she hadn't been expecting that. And they were knowing eyes. Eyes that had perhaps seen too much.

Nicholas Ellis stared straight back at her. So far neither of them had spoken a word, and yet Cathryn had the curious impression that a great deal had already been said. And, instinctively, she knew that she wasn't going to like this man.

CHAPTER TWO

VERY slowly, Cathryn put down her empty coffee-cup. As she did so, Nicholas Ellis came further into the kitchen. He had a pronounced limp, and walked with the help of a stick. The stick had a rubber tip, and so it made as little sound as he did as he moved across to the chair and rather heavily seated himself in it.

'So,' he said at last, in a cool voice, 'you're the nursemaid.'

'I'm the nursemaid,' Cathryn agreed flatly.

At the same time, she took a closer look at his face. He had very little colour, which was hardly surprising after all those weeks in hospital. Cathryn searched for some physical resemblance to his brother and, to her surprise, found it. Not in the eyes, of course. Sir Charles's eyes were hazel, not that unfriendly shade of green. But the more she studied him, the more she realised that this man was a sharper, more vivid image of his older brother. His hair was a little darker, his bone structure more clearly defined, and his mouth fuller, and yet somehow harder.

Nicholas Ellis made himself comfortable in the chair. He propped the stick up within easy reach, and then half raised one dark eyebrow as he saw Cathryn looking at it.

'Are you surprised to find me mobile?' he asked.

'Did you expect me to be on crutches? Or even in a wheelchair?'

'No,' said Cathryn slowly. 'Sir Charles told me that you could walk. Actually, I'm surprised to find you using a stick. I thought you were the type of man who'd refuse to use a prop like that.'

His eyebrow rose even higher. 'We've only just met, Miss Harrison,' he mocked her gently, 'and yet you already think you know the type of man I am?'

'I just thought——' Then she quickly stopped herself. 'I'm sorry,' she said crisply. 'I shouldn't have made such a personal remark. Obviously, you use the stick because you need it.'

'Obviously,' he agreed, his tone giving absolutely nothing away now. 'But you're right, I don't like using it. It's slightly less embarrassing, though, than falling down every time I try to take a few steps.'

'Will you always have a limp?' she asked him.

'Direct, as well as perceptive!' Nicholas Ellis commented. 'But to answer your question, no, I won't always limp. Another few days, and I'll be able to dispense with the stick. A few weeks, and I should be able to walk fairly normally. Do you have any other highly personal questions, Miss Harrison?'

'Not at the moment,' Cathryn replied, somehow managing to keep her own voice even and steady.

'Aren't you even interested in knowing what happened to my last three nursemaids?' he enquired gently, his green eyes suddenly gleaming with sly amusement.

Cathryn gave a deliberately exaggerated sigh. 'I've a feeling that you're going to tell me, whether I want to know or not.'

'I just thought you might find it helpful if you

knew what to expect.' Nicholas's gaze rested on her again, as if assessing her very carefully. 'The first one left because she couldn't cope with my bad temper. My brother tells me that you never lose *your* temper, Miss Harrison. You could find that a very valuable advantage, since I lose mine quite frequently.' He tapped his fingers together lightly, and Cathryn absently noticed that he had scars on the backs of his hands and another, longer one, up his right forearm. 'The second left because she didn't approve of bad language,' he informed her. 'She was a most exasperating girl, and I'm afraid I swore at her quite often.'

'I don't like bad language either,' Cathryn told him calmly. 'But I'm not going to run out of the door the moment you swear at me. And since I've accompanied your brother around plenty of building sites, I doubt if you'll use any words that I haven't heard before.' She allowed a slightly bored expression to cross her face. 'Are you going to tell me about the third girl?'

Nicholas's tone turned silky. 'As in all the best novels, I'm afraid that sex reared its ugly head. She really was quite gorgeous, and I tried to seduce her. Three months in hospital is a *very* long time,' he added meaningfully.

Outwardly, at least, Cathryn managed to remain quite unruffled.

'Since we're going to be living under the same roof for the next couple of weeks, I suppose the question of sex was bound to come up sooner of later,' she said in a deliberately detached tone. 'I didn't think it would be quite so soon, but I suppose we might as well get it out of the way right now. To put it bluntly,

I'm not interested,' she told him very coolly. 'So, as far as I'm concerned, it isn't going to be a problem.'

'Not interested?' repeated Nicholas thoughtfully. 'With me, or not interested in general?'

'Not with you, not with anyone,' Cathryn replied, keeping her face as expressionless as her voice.

Curiosity showed briefly in Nicholas's eyes. Cathryn had the feeling that it was the first genuine emotion that he had shown for a very long time.

'Is this a general dislike, or did something happen to put you off?'

'Who's asking the personal questions now?' she challenged him. 'But, since you want to know, nothing dramatic happened. I tried it and I didn't like it. Some women don't. I only mentioned it because I don't want to have to go through some tiring seduction scene with you.'

'Well, that's honest enough,' he said, to her surprise. 'Why don't we drop the subject, and move on to something else?'

Cathryn was heartily relieved at his suggestion. This was *not* the sort of conversation she had envisaged having with Nicholas Ellis on their first encounter!

'What else do you want to talk about?' she asked.

He shrugged. 'How about telling me exactly how you see your duties over the next couple of weeks? Then I'll know what kind of nursemaid you're going to turn out to be.'

'I am not a nursemaid,' she snapped back at him, her patience suddenly wearing dangerously thin. Perhaps this odd conversation had got to her more than she had realised. 'I'm Sir Charles's personal secretary. I like my job, and right now I'd prefer to be getting on with it! I'm only here as a personal favour to your brother.'

'And what exactly has my brother done to deserve such devoted service?' Nicholas murmured. His eyes narrowed reflectively. 'Would you do *anything* for my brother, Miss Harrison?'

Sir Charles had been right, Cathryn decided. His younger brother *was* quite objectionable!

'No, I wouldn't do anything,' she replied, somehow managing to keep control of her temper. 'And I certainly didn't want to do this!'

'But you're here,' Nicholas pointed out.

'Only because the alternative was that Sir Charles would have had to cancel his trip to America. He refused to go away and leave you on your own.' Cathryn's eyes fixed on him. 'Your brother really does care for you, you know. You might not want to believe it, but I'm sure I'm right.'

'No, I don't believe it. And you're not right.' A strange smile touched the corners of Nicholas Ellis's mouth. 'Don't make pronouncements about something that you can't possibly understand. Just take my word for it when I say that my brother has very little love for me. Whatever he's doing, he's doing out of a sense of duty. Charles was always very strong on duty.'

'And I dare say you were always strong on ingratitude!' Cathryn retaliated. 'And cynicism.'

Nicholas merely shrugged. 'I'm not denying it.' He shifted a little restlessly in his chair. 'We seem to have wandered off the subject. I asked you how you were going to spend the next couple of weeks.'

'Not holding your hand and mopping your brow

whenever it gets a little fevered,' Cathryn shot back at once.

To her astonishment, Nicholas actually grinned. 'You're not a very conventional sort of nursemaid, are you?' he remarked. 'But if you're not going to offer any of the traditional comforts, what are you doing here?'

'I suppose I'm the one who runs for the doctor if you have a sudden relapse. And Sir Charles said you were still taking quite a lot of medication. I'm meant to make sure that you take the right pills at the right time.'

Nicholas's dark eyebrows gently rose. 'And not too many at once?' he suggested.

Cathryn's head shot up. 'Have you ever tried that?' she demanded bluntly. 'An overdose?'

'No, I haven't,' he said, to her intense relief. 'I did take a couple of sleeping pills too many once, but that was entirely an accident. Charles got in rather a flap over it, though. I don't think he was entirely convinced that it wasn't intentional.'

'Are you sure that it wasn't?' Cathryn said suspiciously.

He gave her an unexpectedly relaxed smile. 'I've no desire to leave this world until I absolutely have to. And now we've got that straightened out, why not accept that you're not needed here? I'm quite capable of feeding and caring for myself, and taking the occasional pill—strictly according to prescription, of course,' he added a little mockingly. 'I'm sure that my brother's intentions were very laudable, dragging you over here to look after me, but I don't need you. Go back home and get on with your own life, Miss Harrison.'

It was a very tempting suggestion. More than anything, Cathryn would have loved to have taken him up on it. She had given Sir Charles her word, though. When he returned from America, how could she tell him that she had walked out on his brother after less than an hour?

'I'm sorry,' she said with genuine regret, 'but I can't do that. I'm here for the whole two weeks, so you'd better get used to the idea.'

The relaxation disappeared from Nicholas's features, and instead his green eyes registered intense irritation.

'But I don't want you here,' he said in a very different tone of voice.

'I know you don't,' replied Cathryn, a trifle alarmed by his abrupt change of attitude. 'And I don't want to be here. But there's nothing either of us can do about it, so we'll have to muddle through as best we can.'

It was very obvious that Nicholas Ellis wasn't in the least pleased by her reply. He got to his feet with some difficulty, and then glared down at her.

'I'm beginning to find you very irritating, Miss Harrison.'

Cathryn merely lifted her shoulders in a brief shrug. 'I don't think that your brother expected us to like each other. I suppose the best we can hope for is to tolerate each other's company over the next couple of weeks.'

Nicholas muttered something under his breath and then limped out of the room. Once he had gone, Cathryn let out a deep breath and realised how very tense she had been. Not that she had really expected this first meeting with Sir Charles's brother to be easy. It would have been a minor miracle if they had got on well together from the word go.

She glanced at her watch and then grimaced. It was only mid-morning, and she already felt as if she had been here for hours! And how was she meant to pass the time? She knew some women could have quite happily spent their days cleaning and polishing this elegant flat, and keeping it in pristine condition. Cathryn wasn't in the least domesticated, though. Her own small flat was full of gadgets that were designed to keep housework down to an absolute minimum. And, although she was a reasonable cook when she wanted to be, she didn't want to spend hours in the kitchen. Which left what? Television? Videos? Music? There were plenty of tapes stacked on the shelf in the drawing-room, and she supposed she might have to raid them if she became too bored.

In the end, she decided to make a quick trip to the office after lunch and bring back some work. There was always a backlog waiting to be dealt with, and this would be a perfect opportunity to try and get up to date.

She didn't see any sign of Nicholas for the rest of the morning—which suited her very well. By lunch-time, he still hadn't emerged from his room, and Cathryn wondered if she ought to knock on his door and enquire if he was all right.

In the end, she decided against it. He was probably fine, but just avoiding her. He certainly wouldn't be very pleased if she began poking her nose into his private sanctum so early on during her stay.

She cooked herself an omelette for lunch, ate it, and then cleared away the dishes. Nicholas still hadn't put in an appearance, and Cathryn tapped her fingers together a little worriedly. Didn't the man eat? Surely regular meals were an essential part of any convalescence? There wasn't much flesh on him as it was. Sir Charles wouldn't be very pleased if he came back and found his brother looking positively anorexic!

Cathryn wandered indecisively around the flat for another few minutes. Then she straightened her shoulders and headed directly towards Nicholas's room.

Even as she knocked on his door, she had the feeling that this wasn't a very good idea. And when Nicholas opened it, his green eyes looking totally hostile, she was convinced of that fact.

'What do you want?' he said curtly.

'You haven't had any lunch,' she reminded him.

His features remained extremely cold. 'I'm well aware of that fact. What the hell has it got to do with you?'

Cathryn stared back at him with open dislike. 'I just thought you should have something to eat.'

'Don't start mothering me! It drives me crazy. And don't come knocking on my door every time I'm a few minutes late for a meal. I'll eat when I'm hungry.'

He positively snarled his response at her and Cathryn decided that, from now on, she would let him starve to death, if that was what he wanted.

'Don't worry,' she said in a freezing tone, 'I won't bother you again. And in case you're under any misapprehension, I wasn't offering to cook a meal for you. Since you're so keen to be independent, you can definitely look after yourself.'

'That's very little hardship, since I always do,'

Nicholas informed her, in a slightly more reasonable tone of voice.

Cathryn's delicate eyebrows gently rose. 'Really?' she said, her tone still very cool. 'You surprise me. With all this ultra-macho front you put on, I'd have thought that that sort of thing would have ruined your image.'

Nicholas stared at her in disbelief for a moment. Then his features altered dramatically, and he threw back his head and laughed. It was so unexpected that Cathryn took a couple of steps back. Really, this man was very disconcerting! He switched moods so quickly, and seemed to delight in doing the opposite to what she had been expecting.

'Ultra-macho?' repeated Nicholas, his eyes quite brilliant now with amusement. 'Where on earth did you get that idea from?'

'Maybe from your own publicity,' Cathryn said pointedly. 'I did a little background research on you after Sir Charles asked me to come here. When you're not hopping in and out of trouble-spots all round the world, wearing rather trendy combat gear, you like to hit the social pages with a blonde on your arm— or, sometimes, both arms,' she added, her voice radiating complete disapproval.

Nicholas didn't seem troubled by her accusations. 'When you spend your working life in grim places and even grimmer situations, you need a little light relief when you get home.'

'And nightclubs and blondes fit that bill?' said Cathryn with a sniff.

'Not that it's any of your business, but yes, they do.' She thought he wasn't going to say any more, but to her surprise he went on, 'When I'm working,

I'm often away for weeks or even months at a time. I'm never sure how long I'll be gone, or even if I'll be able to keep in touch. That's a pretty poor basis for any serious relationship. I tried it a couple of times, but each time the girl involved couldn't handle it— and I don't blame her. Now I stick to short-term relationships. That way no one gets hurt.'

'Including you,' Cathryn observed.

'Including me,' he agreed. His smile wasn't quite so pleasant by now. 'Is there any more of my private life I have to explain to you, or are you going to leave me in peace for the rest of the afternoon?'

'Since I'm going out for a while, you'll have all the peace you need,' Cathryn told him. 'I'm going to the office to collect some work. I can't sit around here for two weeks doing nothing.'

'How very conscientious of you,' remarked Nicholas, and there was no trace of laughter left in his eyes. 'But my brother did tell me that you were the perfect secretary.' His gaze slid over her. 'It made me almost curious to meet you. I've never met anyone before who's totally perfect.'

'I do my job, that's all!' she found herself snapping defensively. Then she shut up. This man wasn't going to amuse himself over the next couple of weeks by finding ways of getting under her skin!

'And I'm sure you do it very well.' His green eyes took on a thoughtful expression. 'But then, you're playing for high stakes, aren't you, Cathryn?'

Cathryn stared at him with blank incomprehension. What was the man on about? She didn't know, and she decided that she didn't care. She didn't have to understand him, or even make more than a cursory effort to be pleasant to him. She just had to make sure that he stayed in reasonably good health over the next couple of weeks.

'I'll be leaving for the office in about half an hour. I won't be gone for long,' she informed him. 'You will be all right on your own, won't you?'

'I'll try to survive,' he said caustically. Then he closed the door in her face.

With an effort, Cathryn controlled her own heated reaction. 'You have to make allowances for him,' she muttered under her breath. 'He's been through a traumatic time. His nerves are still on edge.'

Yet her own usually steady nerves weren't feeling any too healthy, and she was glad to get out of Sir Charles's flat. She took a taxi to the office, and spent far longer than was necessary sorting out work that could be done at home. When she couldn't spin it out any longer, she gathered together the files, collected a portable electric typewriter from one of the other offices, and then very reluctantly headed back to the flat.

She had to ring the bell several times before Nicholas finally opened it. 'I know you've got a limp, but I think you could have opened the door a bit quicker,' she said crossly, dumping the typewriter in the hall and letting the heavy files drop on to a nearby table.

'I was working,' he said briefly. 'You interrupted me.'

Cathryn glanced up. 'Working? On what?' Then she flushed slightly. 'All right, I know. It's none of my business.'

'No, it isn't,' he agreed. 'But it isn't any great secret. I've had an offer from a publisher to write a book about the events leading up to the moment when I ran my Jeep over a land-mine.' He said it so matter-of-factly that it was hard to figure out if he was finding it an effort to keep his tone so light. 'I've got to get it finished by the end of the month, though. The public have notoriously bad memories. At the moment, they're still interested because the whole thing is relatively fresh in their minds. Leave it too long, and they won't want to know about it.'

Cathryn wrinkled her nose. 'You're going to write about getting blown up? I think that's pretty ghoulish!'

'Perhaps it is,' he said in an unconcerned voice. 'But it should make me some money.'

Cathryn recalled something Sir Charles had said about Nicholas not being able to afford a private nurse.

'You're short of cash?' she said curiously. 'But surely you earn a good salary?'

'Reasonably good. But by the time I've paid for a flat in central London, a car, and various other expenses, there isn't a great deal left.'

'But don't you have a private income?'

The words popped out before she could stop them. Too late, she realised she was straying on to dangerously personal ground again, and nervously waited for Nicholas to tell her that in no uncertain terms.

Instead, though, he looked at her thoughtfully. 'What exactly do you mean by that?'

'Just that—well, you come from a wealthy family, don't you?' she said rather uncomfortably.

'You mean, my brother has money coming out of his ears, so why don't I?' said Nicholas softly. 'To begin with, I didn't start out with as much as Charles. Being the elder son, he took the title, the family home, and a sizeable chunk of the estate. The assets that were left were then split equally between us. Charles used his share to set himself up in business, and he's been flourishing ever since. My part of the inheritance disappeared in a rather different direction, though. If Charles were here, he'd probably tell you that I squandered it.'

'Squandered it on what?' Cathryn couldn't stop herself from asking.

A rather strange look came over Nicholas's face. 'How about gambling debts?' he suggested.

Her eyes opened much wider. 'You gambled away your inheritance? *All* of it?'

'Every single penny.' His mouth curled into a self-mocking smile. 'I can see from the look on your face that you don't approve.'

'Of course I don't!'

'One more thing on which you and my brother see eye to eye,' Nicholas remarked. 'He didn't approve, either.' His green eyes glinted at her. 'You and Charles really do seem to be very compatible. Two minds that think alike on so many things. Including your opinion of me, no doubt.'

'You're certainly right about that!' Cathryn gathered together her files. 'I'm going to get on with some work,' she informed him sharply. 'I'll use the drawing-room, if that won't inconvenience you.'

'As long as you keep out of my way as much as possible, you shouldn't be too much of a nuisance. Although I don't somehow think you'll be staying the full two weeks, Miss Harrison,' he added pointedly.

'You might have a reputation for being difficult, Mr Ellis,' Cathryn replied in a haughty tone, 'but believe me, I simply find you tiresome. And I'm more than capable of coping with whatever tantrums you might choose to throw.'

With that, she swept through the nearest doorway, and was pleased at being able to make such an impressive exit. It helped to compensate for the fact that her heart was thumping and her knees felt distinctly weak.

She set the portable typewriter up on the table near the window, and worked through what was left of the afternoon. Around half-past five, she could hear Nicholas moving around in the kitchen, and she waited until he had gone back to his own room before going to get herself something to eat.

She watched television for a couple of hours during the evening, but she couldn't seem to concentrate on any of the programmes. Around ten, she decided to have an early night. The day had proved even more exhausting than she had expected and she certainly wasn't looking forward to tomorrow.

The bed was warm and comfortable, and Cathryn fell asleep just a couple of minutes after crawling between the sheets. She woke up some time later with a start, though, and stared into the darkness, wondering what had woken her. Then she heard someone shouting. With pulses beating far faster than usual, she sat up.

'It must be someone outside,' she told herself rather shakily. In an exclusive residential area like this, though, it was highly unlikely that someone would be causing a disturbance in the street.

Cathryn switched on the lamp beside the bed. Her watch told her it was half-past two in the morning, and she felt very wide awake. Her pulses were slowing down again now and, with a small sigh, she swung herself out of bed and wriggled into a dressing-gown. She supposed she ought to have a look around, to check that everything was all right.

The carpet under her bare feet was so thick that she didn't make a single sound as she made her way through the flat. It was very quiet everywhere now. She still didn't know what had caused that disturbance, but it seemed to be over.

She decided she might as well have a hot drink now she was up, and headed towards the kitchen. As she opened the door, she found the light was already on, and she paused in the doorway.

Inside, Nicholas was sitting at the table with his back to her. His head and shoulders were slumped, and he obviously hadn't heard her approach.

Rather nervously, Cathryn cleared her throat. The small sound made him jump violently; then he swung round to face her, eyes blazing.

'What the hell are you doing, creeping up on me like that?' he demanded furiously.

Cathryn shrugged apologetically. 'The carpets in this flat are so thick that it's difficult *not* to creep. Sorry if I startled you.'

'What are you doing up?' he asked curtly.

'I heard someone shouting. I wondered what was going on.'

'It was me,' Nicholas replied, after a short pause. 'I had a bad dream. I didn't mean to disturb you.'

She came a little further into the kitchen. 'Do you get dreams like that often?'

'Less often than I did at first.' He lifted his shoulders briefly. 'According to the doctors, it's the delayed shock still working its way out of my system. Eventually, they should stop altogether.'

As Cathryn moved closer, she noticed a bottle of spirits in front of him.

'I don't think you should drink,' she said disapprovingly. 'Not when you're taking all those pills.'

'Sometimes a few drinks are all that get me through the night,' he growled. 'And I don't take *that* many pills.'

Cathryn looked at him sceptically. 'There seem to be enough bottles of them lined up in the bathroom. I don't know what half of them are for, but I'm pretty certain most of them don't mix well with alcohol.'

His green gaze fixed on her. 'What I do to my body is my affair,' he told her softly.

'Not while I'm here,' Cathryn replied promptly. 'That's one of the reasons your brother wanted me to stay—to stop you from doing anything stupid.'

Nicholas got heavily to his feet and then stood facing her. Although Cathryn certainly didn't like the look on his face, she stood her ground without flinching.

'I don't need my brother's secretary to tell me what I can or can't do,' he said, his tone suddenly quite deadly. 'Am I getting through to you?'

She felt her throat go dry, but still didn't back away.

'Any idiot knows that you shouldn't mix pills and drink,' she insisted stubbornly. 'For all I know, you might be planning on taking a couple of sleeping pills on top of that lot, and that really *would* be dangerous.'

'What an interfering little bitch you are!' he said unpleasantly. 'What makes you think you've got the right to come charging in like this, telling me how to run my life?'

'Your brother——' began Cathryn.

'Ah, yes, my brother,' interrupted Nicholas. 'By all means, let's bring my brother into this. After all, you wouldn't even be here if it weren't for him, would you, Miss Harrison?'

'I certainly wouldn't,' she said with some fervour.

His eyes took on an expression that sent small shivers right through her nervous system.

'And why exactly are you so anxious to please my brother?' he enquired with open malice.

'I work for him,' Cathryn answered, and knew that her voice betrayed the deep unease that he was beginning to arouse in her.

'Of course,' he agreed smoothly. 'But don't you think this particular job rather goes outside the usual terms of employment?'

'I suppose so. But I agreed to do it as a special favour.' Even as she said it, Cathryn knew she had chosen the wrong words. It hadn't come out at all the way she had intended. From the look on Nicholas's face, though, it was obviously what he had been expecting to hear.

'A special favour,' he repeated, his mouth setting into a line of harsh amusement. 'What a tactful way of putting it.' Before Cathryn could indignantly demand what he meant by that, he went on, 'Why don't you tell me a little about your social life, Miss Harrison? Do you have a boyfriend? Or someone you live with?'

The sudden change of tack threw her momentarily off balance. 'I don't see that it's anything to do with you,' she spluttered. 'But the answer's no to both questions.'

She realised at once that she shouldn't have

answered at all. She *wouldn't* have done if he hadn't so thoroughly managed to unsettle her.

'I rather thought that's what you'd say.' The grim amusement spread from his mouth to his eyes. 'You don't strike me as the sort of girl who would go out with just anyone. You would want to wait until exactly the *right* person came along.'

Cathryn somehow recovered a little of her composure. 'I've had enough of this,' she said coldly. 'I'm going back to my room.'

Nicholas took a couple of steps forward, moving with unexpected speed considering his injured leg.

'Before you go, I'd like to try a little experiment,' he said silkily.

Before Cathryn had a chance to ask him what he was talking about, he slid one arm smoothly around her waist and pulled her towards him. The sudden physical contact was so unexpected that she froze instead of struggling free. And that was her first mistake, because by the time she had recovered it was too late to break away from him.

Her second mistake was not turning her head away quickly enough as his warm lips descended on hers. Although she frantically tried to free her mouth, he simply moved with her, his lips pursuing hers with ruthless intent.

Despite his months in hospital, he was still a lot stronger than she was. And through the stifling closeness of him Cathryn became aware that his attack on her was quite deliberately sensual. Any other woman might have found herself beginning to succumb to the undeniably expert pressure of his mouth and the clever movements of his hands. She managed to keep her responses frozen, though.

'I'm not getting through to you?' Nicholas murmured under his breath. 'Somehow, I expected that. But I suppose it's worth one more try. . .'

This time, he eased back a little, and his assault on her became more subtle.

His tongue eased its way between her tight lips, despite all her efforts to stop him, and languidly licked the inner warmth of her mouth. The breath caught in Cathryn's throat because the intrusion wasn't as unpleasant as she had expected it to be.

As if aware of her surprise, he immediately followed up his very small advantage, searching for other points of vulnerability. His fingers caressed the swell of her breast with a familiarity which aroused fresh indignation in her, and he didn't seem to care that the pressure of his body was quite blatantly betraying his own rapid arousal.

With an enormous effort, Cathryn finally managed to wrench her head free. 'Stop it!' she yelled. 'Stop it *at once!*'

To her astonishment, he immediately let go of her.

'What the hell do you think you're doing?' she demanded furiously.

'Just proving a point,' Nicholas replied calmly.

'What sort of point did you think you could prove by behaving like that?' Cathryn was still snarling at him, and Nicholas raised one dark eyebrow.

'You'd better get control of yourself, or you'll ruin your reputation for never losing your temper,' he warned.

'Perhaps I've never lost my temper because I've never been in this sort of situation before!' Her eyes blazed at him stormily. 'Did you really think you could seduce me?'

'I was fairly certain that I couldn't,' replied Nicholas, his own voice remaining infuriatingly calm.

'Then why go through that ridiculous charade?'

'I suppose I just wanted to confirm that I was right.'

'About what?' she challenged him.

'Your rather unbelievable lack of interest in sex. Of course you don't want to go to bed with me—or with anyone else,' Nicholas stated with cold precision. 'You're saving yourself for my brother, aren't you, Miss Harrison?'

CHAPTER THREE

CATHRYN didn't even bother to deny his incredible accusation. Instead, she stalked out of the kitchen, marched directly to her own bedroom, slammed the door very noisily behind her, and then sat on the bed practically gibbering with pure rage.

How *dared* he say such a thing? Sir Charles was a very attractive man, and highly eligible on all counts, but she had never once thought of him in that way. Her heart refused to flutter when he walked into the room, no sparks jumped between them whenever he came near, and she was sure they never would. They worked together, she felt comfortable with him, and that was it.

She eventually crawled back into bed, but she couldn't sleep. She was still seething inside, and she felt a totally uncharacteristic desire to do Nicholas Ellis some actual physical harm.

Around dawn, she gave up trying to sleep and decided to make herself a drink. She padded back to the kitchen, and then paused at the door for a moment. What if Nicholas was still there?

What if he was? she told herself angrily. *He* was the one who ought to be feeling utterly ashamed of himself—although she very much doubted whether he ever experienced such an emotion.

She shoved open the door, and then let out an involuntary sigh of relief when she found the kitchen was empty. She heated up some water and made herself some coffee. When she sat at the table to drink it, though, she found herself staring at the bottle of whisky which Nicholas had been drinking from the night before.

The level seemed to have dropped considerably, and Cathryn scowled at it. She hoped he woke up with an absolutely appalling hangover. Or, better still, was quite comatose. That would mean she wouldn't have to listen to his malicious tongue for a while!

Just as she finished her coffee, the door opened and Nicholas wandered in. He was leaning heavily on his stick, but apart from that seemed to be in annoyingly good health. His eyes were clear and his hand perfectly steady as he poured himself some coffee.

'I thought you'd be taking it black,' Cathryn remarked pointedly as he added some milk.

'It takes more than a couple of large whiskies to give me a hangover,' he answered in an unperturbed voice. Then he looked at her with some interest. 'I'm surprised you're still talking to me,' he added. 'After last night, I rather expected you to flounce out of the flat at the first possible opportunity.'

'Which goes to show how little you know about me,' Cathryn replied with a coolness that was definitely only on the surface. 'Just because you like to play rather childish games, it doesn't follow that I like to do the same.'

Nicholas's expression became thoughtful. 'That chill's back in your voice again,' he remarked. 'If you're as cold inside as you can be on the outside, it's not surprising that you don't like sex. It needs some warmth and giving to be good. You don't seem to have much of a talent for either of those things.'

Cathryn instantly bristled. 'Just because I didn't enjoy being jumped on last night——' she began fiercely.

'I didn't jump on you,' Nicholas interrupted calmly. 'If I had, you'd have known it,' he finished meaningfully.

'Whatever you like to call it, it was completely unnecessary and unpleasant,' she snapped back at him. 'And it certainly wasn't enough to make me turn tail and run, if that was your intention. You said that your brother has a sense of duty. Well, so do I. I gave my word to Sir Charles that I'd stay here for the entire two weeks, and that's precisely what I intend to do. I'd prefer it if there weren't any more incidents like last night, but if there are I'm sure I can cope with them. After all, I realise that I have to make allowances for you,' she added, not caring in the least that she was now being deliberately insulting. 'Sir Charles did warn me that your accident had left you mentally unstable.'

For the briefest of moments, a gleam of pure fire shone in Nicholas's green eyes. Then the flare disappeared completely, to be replaced by a rather ominous calm.

'Since you've introduced the subject of my brother, perhaps there are one or two things I ought to warn you about concerning him,' he drawled. 'For a start, he might think you're the perfect secretary, but that's all you're ever going to be, as far as he's concerned.'

Cathryn's own eyes became frosty. 'That's all I want to be.'

Nicholas raised one eyebrow in flagrant disbelief.

'Really?' Then he gave a thoroughly unpleasant smile. 'You must think I'm very naïve, Miss Harrison.'

'I've no idea *what* you are,' she retaliated instantly. 'And I really don't care in the least. I simply want to get through the next couple of weeks with as few problems as possible, and then get on with my normal life.'

'And what exactly does your day usually consist of?' Nicholas enquired in a caustic tone. 'Parading yourself in front of my brother in various fetching outfits? Trying very hard to be completely indispensable? Hoping that *this* will be the day when he finally notices what a lot you've got going for you?' His gaze slid over her with deliberate slowness. 'And you do have a great deal going for you, Miss Harrison,' he said in a voice that had become slightly husky. 'Thick chestnut hair—it probably looks sensational when you wear it loose. Great tawny eyes,' he went on, continuing his inventory, much to her furious embarrassment, 'a face that's all the more interesting for being not quite beautiful, and a *very* nice body. And it's all very subtle, which makes it even more attractive. You're not a knock-'em-dead-at-first-sight sort of girl. You're the kind of girl who could slowly grow on a man—but you're not going to grow on my brother,' he warned. 'There's only ever been one woman in Charles's life, and that was his wife. He might have been damned lonely and miserable since she died, but he won't ever want to replace her.'

Cathryn was so disgusted by his accusation that she was chasing after his brother that she didn't even bother to reply. She wasn't going to get into any more degrading arguments on this subject. Let him think what he liked! It didn't matter in the least to her. Two more weeks, and she wouldn't even have to see him again.

She began to get herself some breakfast. As she moved around the kitchen, Nicholas sat and watched her. For a while, she tried to ignore it. Then it finally began to get on her nerves.

'Are you going to sit and watch me all morning?' she snapped.

He shrugged easily. 'Why not? I've nothing more interesting to do.'

'You could get on with your book,' she retorted. Anything to get him out of here! There was something about that green gaze that set her teeth on edge. 'Didn't you say your publisher had set a deadline?'

'Yes, he has. But I don't know if I'm going to meet it.'

'Why not? You've plenty of free time on your hands. There's really no excuse for not getting on with it.'

'Except the mental blocks inside my head. I'd prefer to forget these last few months, rather than relive the whole thing on paper.'

For just an instant, Cathryn felt an entirely unexpected pang of sympathy for him. Then she remembered how very unsympathetic he had been towards *her*, and her attitude swiftly hardened again.

'If you hadn't gambled away your inheritance, you wouldn't be short of money and *need* to write the book,' she reminded him.

Nicholas quickly raised his head and seemed about to make a very sharp reply. Then he visibly stopped himself, and instead gave a curt nod. 'I dare say you're right.'

Cathryn hadn't expected him to accept her blunt statement without some kind of retaliation. She gave a faint frown. There was something here that wasn't quite right. For a few moments, she wondered what it was. Then she decided that she really wasn't interested and she carried on getting her breakfast.

When she finally glanced in his direction again, she found he had gone. Cathryn blinked. She had never known anyone who could move so silently! Despite the fact that he still had to use a stick, he seemed to be able to move around without making a single sound. It was rather unnerving, because it meant that she could never be sure when he was creeping up on her.

She ate breakfast, and then headed towards the bathroom. A brisk shower helped her to put her disturbed night behind her—although she certainly wasn't going to forget those outrageous suggestions Nicholas had made about her and Sir Charles! She dressed fairly casually, in a skirt and light jumper instead of the rather severe suits that she wore to the office, and brushed out the thick chestnut mass of her hair.

Since she planned to spend the morning working, she wandered along to the drawing-room and sorted through the files she had brought from the office yesterday. She had to admit that, for some reason, she didn't feel in the mood for work. Since it had to be done, though, she sat down and forced herself to get on with it.

Mid-morning, she pushed the files to one side and set off for the kitchen, to make some coffee. As she passed Nicholas's door she could hear the muffled sound of typing. Cathryn gave a slightly grim smile. It looked as if he, too, was forcing himself to get down to work. Natural courtesy made her stop for a moment and raise her hand to tap on his door. She intended to ask if he wanted some coffee. Then she drew back her hand at the last moment, and her brows drew together in a determined line. No, she *wasn't* going to wait on him. That wasn't what she was here for, and anyway, he certainly wouldn't appreciate it. Let him get his own meals and drinks!

Cathryn wasn't usually so hard-hearted, but then, she had never come up against anyone quite like Nicholas Ellis before. And she would be more than pleased if she never did again!

She worked on through the day, only stopping for a light lunch. By the end of the afternoon, pleased with the amount of work she had accomplished, she stretched her rather stiff limbs. If she carried on at this pace, she would be finished by the end of tomorrow.

The sound of the doorbell ringing made her turn her head. As far as she knew, no visitors were expected at the flat.

She waited for Nicholas to answer the door. When the bell kept ringing, she sighed in irritation. All right, so the man had a limp and couldn't be expected to dash about like a sprinter. He seemed to get around perfectly well when he wanted to, though!

The doorbell rang again, even more insistently, and Cathryn hauled herself to her feet.

'Take your finger off the bell! I'm *coming*,' she grumbled under her breath.

She hurried across the hall and opened the front

door. Then she blinked in surprise as she found herself looking at a tall, willowy blonde.

The blonde seemed equally surprised to see her. 'Er—have I got the right address?' she said in a rather breathless little voice. 'I'm looking for Nicholas. Nicholas Ellis,' she finished helpfully.

'You've got the right address,' Cathryn confirmed. 'Is he expecting you?'

The blonde gave her a dazzling smile. 'Not really. I thought I'd surprise him.'

Cathryn rather cynically thought to herself that this was the sort of surprise every man secretly dreamed of!

'I suppose you'd better come in,' she said, and held the door open as the girl glided in, somehow managing to walk very gracefully even though she was wearing impossibly high heels. Expensive perfume saturated the air as she drifted past Cathryn, and the soft leather skirt she was wearing must have cost a minor fortune.

This was definitely a very up-market blonde! Cathryn decided with a marked lift of her eyebrows. Not the sort that she would have expected Nicholas to go for—just too *obvious*—but men constantly surprised her with their choice of women.

'I'll tell Nicholas that you're here,' Cathryn said. She opened the door to the drawing-room. 'You'd better wait in there.'

While the blonde slunk sexily through the door and draped herself over the sofa, Cathryn went along to Nicholas's room and knocked briskly on the door.

The tapping of typewriter keys stopped for a moment.

'Go away, I'm working,' Nicholas called out

tersely. Then she could hear the typewriter going again.

'You've got a visitor,' she informed him.

'I don't want to see anyone.'

'I think you might change your mind when you see her,' Cathryn remarked wryly.

The typing stopped again. A few moments later his door opened.

'Her?' Nicholas demanded, with a dark scowl. 'Who the hell's turned up?'

'I don't know. She didn't give her name. But once you see her you're bound to recognise her. She isn't the sort of girl you'd easily forget,' Cathryn finished pointedly.

Nicholas was still scowling, though. 'I know a lot of girls like that.' Then, when he saw the look on Cathryn's face, a dry smile touched his mouth. 'Most of the time, I meet them during the course of work. I don't go round personally collecting them.'

'Well, this one doesn't look as if she's anything to do with work. Not unless you're in a very exotic line of business,' she finished, her own mouth breaking into a faint grin.

Nicholas looked at her with new interest. 'That must be the first time you've smiled since you arrived here,' he commented.

'Never mind about that,' Cathryn said, unexpectedly confused by the personal remark. 'Just go and deal with this girl. I've dumped her in the drawing-room.'

For a moment, he looked as if he was going to refuse. Then he gave a rather exaggerated sigh and limped off down the hall.

Cathryn made her way to the kitchen. She would

make herself some coffee, which would give Nicholas time to get rid of his visitor. Then she would clear away the work that she had left spread all over the table in the drawing-room.

A few moments later, though, she realised that some of the papers she had left lying around were fairly confidential. She ought to clear them away right now, before Nicholas or that girl got a chance to look at them. She didn't suppose that either of them were particularly interested in Sir Charles's business affairs, but as his personal secretary it was her duty to make sure that his private papers *remained* private.

Rather hurriedly, she made her way back to the drawing-room. It didn't cross her mind for one moment that she should knock before going in. She swept into the room, and then stopped dead as she found herself confronted by the sight of Nicholas and the blonde wrapped around each other.

Neither of them seemed to have heard her come in. Cathryn coughed very loudly. At the same time, she tried not to feel totally embarrassed. If anything, *they* were the ones who ought to feel awkward, she argued fiercely with herself.

'It's all right, Miss Harrison, I do know that you're there,' murmured Nicholas, without even turning round.

If he knew she was there, why didn't he let go of the blonde for just a few moments? she muttered to herself with growing irritation. All she wanted to do was to collect the files together, and then get out of here. It wouldn't take more than a minute; then they could get up to whatever they wanted.

Then it slowly dawned on her that it was the

blonde who was wrapped around Nicholas, rather than the other way round. In fact, Nicholas was looking slightly trapped, as if this slinky blonde was rather more than he could cope with in his present state of health.

Cathryn suddenly felt like chuckling to herself. She liked seeing Nicholas Ellis at a slight disadvantage, for once.

'I just came to collect some papers,' she told them crisply, walking towards the table. 'I'll be out of here in a few moments.'

The blonde seemed to have been thrown a little off balance by Cathryn's unexpected arrival. She unwound herself from Nicholas and slunk back on to the sofa, looking more than a little put out.

'Perhaps I ought to introduce the two of you,' Nicholas suggested. 'Miss Harrison, this is Mandy.'

Mandy looked up at Nicholas, completely ignoring Cathryn. 'I suppose she's some sort of housekeeper?' she said in a bored tone.

'Actually, she's my nursemaid,' Nicholas said, slightly mockingly.

'Well, whatever she is—do you think she could get me a cup of tea?'

Cathryn didn't wait for Nicholas to reply. 'I don't run around after Nicholas, so I'm certainly not going to run around after you,' she said evenly. 'The kitchen's at the end of the hall. If you want some tea, go and make it yourself.'

She rather enjoyed the way that Mandy's delectable mouth fell open in blank surprise. Before the blonde girl could think of an equally crushing reply—and Cathryn guessed that that would take her some time—she collected together her files and made a dignified exit from the room.

Once outside, she wasn't sure whether to laugh or be angry. In the end, she decided that it wasn't worth getting worked up over Mandy. Cathryn gave a wry shrug, and headed back to her own room.

She spent some time sorting the files into order, and then realised she was getting hungry. As she made her way to the kitchen, she could hear the murmur of voices coming from the drawing-room, and guessed that Nicholas was still fully occupied with Mandy. Cathryn just hoped that his health was up to it!

She prepared her evening meal, and took it back to her bedroom on a tray. There was a small portable television in her room, so she watched that while she ate. Then, tiring of the rather bland programmes, she read for a couple of hours. Later in the evening she decided to take a bath. She pinned her hair loosely on top of her head, grabbed a towelling robe and her bag of toiletries, and headed for the bathroom.

Ten minutes later, she was soaking blissfully in hot, scented water. Gradually, she felt herself beginning to unwind as the heat relaxed her muscles. Showers were fine when you needed to wash, but there was nothing like a bath for getting all the kinks out of your nervous system.

Half an hour passed peacefully, and she still didn't feel in the least inclined to get out of the bath. She had topped up the water a couple of times, so it was still deliciously hot, and she could feel herself becoming drowsy. This had been a good idea, she told herself. After this, she would sleep like a log tonight.

In fact, she would have to be careful that she didn't fall asleep right here and now!

Her eyes had actually begun to droop sleepily when a sharp knock on the door made them fly open again.

'Who is it?' she demanded. Then she realised that was a ridiculous question. There was only one person it *could* be.

'Are you going to stay in there all night?' came Nicholas's slightly curt enquiry.

'And what if I am?' Cathryn retorted huffily. She could feel her sense of relaxation beginning to evaporate, and that annoyed her. It had taken her a long while to get rid of all the tension that seemed to build up after any encounter with Nicholas Ellis. Now, just when she had managed it, he was getting her strung up all over again!

'Mandy would like to take a bath,' he announced.

'*What*? Wait there a moment,' she snapped.

She heaved herself out of the hot water and wriggled her wet body into the towelling robe. Then she hurried over to the door, leaving a trail of wet footprints and drips.

She quickly unlocked and opened it; then she glared at Nicholas as he stood calmly outside.

'What do you mean, Mandy wants to take a bath? Surely she's got a bath of her own at home?'

'Of course she has,' Nicholas agreed. 'But she's decided to stay here tonight.'

Cathryn suddenly remembered the large shoulder-bag that the blonde girl had been carrying. Mandy must have planned to stay from the very start, bringing with her everything she would need. And

Cathryn could guess what that list included. Expensive bath oils, a change of sexy underwear, and something very slinky to wear—or perhaps, not to wear!—in bed tonight.

On the other hand, it was none of her business how Nicholas spent his time—or rather, *misspent* it. For some reason, Cathryn had taken an immediate dislike to Mandy, but she could quite see that a healthy male would look at the blonde girl from a very different point of view. Even a physically below-par male, such as Nicholas, would be distracted from his medical problems for a few hours.

Cathryn pulled her wet robe more tightly around her still dripping body. 'Mandy will have to wait until I'm finished in here,' she said, not caring in the least that her voice radiated disapproval. 'Then she can have the bathroom for the rest of the night, if she wants it.'

'How very generous of you,' Nicholas remarked. An amused glitter lit his eyes now, and he seemed in an unexpectedly good mood. Cathryn wasn't particularly surprised. What male *wouldn't* be in a good mood, with someone like Mandy waiting for him?

She closed and relocked the door; then she peeled off the damp bathrobe. Slowly, she dried herself on one of Sir Charles's huge fluffy towels. Then she found herself taking a mental inventory of her own body.

Medium height, good legs, slim hips, firm breasts—when it was all put together, it was certainly enough to draw glances whenever she walked into a room. On the other hand, she definitely wasn't in the same league as Mandy. Men wouldn't just look at Mandy—their eyes would positively pop out!

Cathryn gave a faint sigh. It seemed rather unfair that sex appeal—or whatever you wanted to call it— was handed out in such varying quantities. Some girls had far too much of it, while others just seemed to have missed out altogether. She supposed she came somewhere in the middle, which was OK until you met someone like Mandy, and realised that girls who had lashings of it definitely had an unfair advantage over all the others.

Then Cathryn's brows drew together as she realised that her thoughts had been wandering in a direction which they had never really taken before. Why was she suddenly feeling so inadequate, when she knew perfectly well that she wasn't?

'Blonde bimbo!' she snorted irritably under her breath. 'I wouldn't *want* to be like that, even if I had the choice.'

In a thoroughly unsettled mood, she finished drying herself, slapped scented body lotion over her warm skin, and wriggled into her nightshirt. Then she picked up her damp robe, grabbed hold of her toiletry bag, and left the bathroom free for Mandy.

Back in her own room, she slumped on to the bed and watched television for a while. A late film was on, but it didn't hold her attention. In the end, she decided to make herself a hot drink, and then try to get some sleep.

She went along to the kitchen, made some coffee, and was just wandering back to her bedroom when she saw the bathroom door open.

Mandy came out, wafting scent in all directions and wearing a flimsy silk and lace concoction that would have got even an octogenarian's pulse racing.

'Oh—hello,' she said vaguely, not even looking

directly at Cathryn. 'I didn't know you slept in. I don't suppose you'll disturb us, though, will you?'

Cathryn gritted her teeth. 'I'll certainly try not to.'

Mandy gave another empty smile. 'Good. See you in the morning.'

'You're sure you wouldn't like breakfast in bed?' Cathryn couldn't stop herself from enquiring sarcastically.

'That would be very nice,' Mandy called over her shoulder as she drifted off. 'Just tea and a slice of toast, please.'

Cathryn stared after her in disbelief. She had actually thought Cathryn had meant it! How dumb was it possible to be?

Mandy wandered on in the direction of Nicholas's bedroom, but Cathryn didn't wait to see her go through the door. She went back to her own room, shut the door far more noisily than was necessary, and then settled down to watch the last half of the film with fierce concentration.

She didn't sleep well and blamed it on the fact that she had made the coffee too strong. She finally managed to doze for a couple of hours just before dawn, but woke again just as the sun was rising. Her eyes felt bleary, and her head ached slightly from lack of sleep. With a faint groan, she hauled herself out of bed and shuffled towards the kitchen.

Early though it was, Nicholas had still got there before her.

And he wasn't just up. He was looking unexpectedly bright-eyed. After a night with Mandy, Cathryn had expected to find him in urgent need of resuscitation!

'Want some coffee?' he offered. 'I've just made

some.' Then, when she didn't reply, his green gaze studied her thoughtfully. 'Why are you looking at me like that?'

Her eyebrows lifted expressively. 'I suppose I'm just not used to your being so polite. Maybe Mandy's a good influence on you,' she commented drily.

'Mandy is a thorough nuisance,' he stated, to her complete astonishment. 'And I certainly didn't invite her round here. In fact, I hardly know the girl.'

'Hardly know her?' Cathryn echoed in disbelief. 'She wanders into your bedroom at midnight, wearing not much more than a splash of perfume, and you expect me to believe you hardly know her?' Then, to her annoyance, she found herself flushing. She hadn't meant to let him know that she had seen Mandy going to his room. She didn't approve of casual sex, but it was entirely his affair if he wanted to risk indulging in it.

'If you'd watched a little longer, you'd also have seen Mandy leave my room,' Nicholas told her, apparently fairly unperturbed by her outburst. 'Mandy is a rather frustrated little girl this morning.'

'You turned her away?' Cathryn couldn't quite keep the incredulity out of her voice.

Nicholas grinned, confusing her further. He was in a good temper so very rarely that she didn't know quite how to cope with this side of him.

'I turned her away,' he agreed. 'On purely medical grounds,' he added, his eyes glinting.

'What medical grounds?' Cathryn demanded. Then she found herself flushing brightly again. 'All right,' she said irritably, annoyed by her lack of control over the colour that kept surging over her hot cheekbones, 'I know it's nothing to do with me.'

'No, it isn't,' he agreed, in that same unruffled tone. 'But I'll tell you anyway, since you're so interested. The doctors have advised me to avoid any unnecessary excitement over the next few weeks. And Mandy can be *very* exciting,' he softly purred.

'If you're meant to avoid excitement, why did you kiss *me* the other night?' Cathryn demanded. 'You seemed pretty excited on that occasion,' she reminded him pointedly.

He lifted his shoulders in amused acceptance. 'I told you—three months in hospital is a very long time. It's very hard not to give in to temptation. But I am trying to follow doctors' orders. And they've recommended that I live like a monk for the next three or four weeks.'

Cathryn stared at him. 'Then you really mean that——?'

'I mean that Mandy was extremely disappointed,' he said with a mocking smile. 'It also means that she'll be leaving as soon as I've been along to drag her out of bed.'

'Will she want to go?'

'No, she won't. But she's already outstayed her welcome.'

Cathryn looked at him curiously. 'How on earth did you get involved with someone like Mandy?' Then she realised that she was asking personal questions again. Was he going to order her to mind her own business?

He did no such thing, though. Instead, to her surprise, he answered her question. 'I met Mandy through a mutual friend. I took her out one evening, but once was enough. She hasn't got a brain in her gorgeous little head. I've met plenty of blondes who are bright and intelligent, but Mandy certainly isn't one of them!'

But Cathryn wasn't at all sure that she swallowed that story. 'If you only took her out once, why did she turn up on the doorstep like that?' she demanded.

'Mandy likes celebrities,' Nicholas said simply. 'For some reason, it makes her feel important to be seen around with someone who's well known. Since I've appeared on the television, and then attracted even more attention by getting myself blown up, she's decided that I fall into the celebrity category. And once Mandy gets hold of a celebrity, she doesn't let go of him easily.'

Cathryn considered what he had said for a few moments. 'That's rather sad,' she said at last.

Nicholas looked faintly surprised. 'Yes, it is,' he agreed. 'But I didn't expect you to see it that way.'

'Why not?'

'Women often seem to feel threatened by someone like Mandy. All that sex appeal on blatant display makes them feel uneasy, indignant—perhaps even inadequate.'

Cathryn was about to deny it quite furiously when she suddenly remembered her own reaction yesterday. 'Perhaps you're right,' she admitted at last, with deep reluctance.

'Not that you've anything to worry about,' Nicholas went on, in the same slightly detached tone. 'When it comes to sex appeal, you've got a lot going for you. Not quite like Mandy, of course—women like Mandy are a fairly rare species,' he continued drily. 'But you could certainly turn me on, if you put your mind to it.'

Another of those infuriating flushes spread across her face. 'I've no intention of putting my mind to it,' she informed him hotly.

He gave an unconcerned shrug. 'I didn't for one moment think that you would. I'm just saying that you *could*, if you really wanted to. And don't give me that spiel about not being interested in sex,' he went on as she opened her mouth indignantly. 'Some women aren't, I'm willing to accept that. Just as some men find it easy—or even prefer—to be celibate. But you're not one of them, Cathryn.' It was the first time he had used her Christian name, and the way he said it made her feel distinctly uneasy. 'There's a light in your eyes sometimes. And you move quite seductively, although I don't think you know you're doing it—which, incidentally, makes it all the more provocative. No, there's nothing basically cold or frigid about you,' he finished thoughtfully. 'Some day, someone's going to prove that to you.'

But Cathryn had had quite enough of this conversation. 'Perhaps they will, and perhaps they won't,' she retorted, getting swiftly to her feet. 'Personally, I very much doubt it. I *know* what I am. But whoever proves it one way or the other, that person isn't going to be *you*.'

Then she flounced out of the kitchen before he could make any more of his highly unsettling observations.

CHAPTER FOUR

HALFWAY through the morning, Cathryn heard Mandy leave the flat. A couple of minutes later, Nicholas came limping into the drawing-room looking much relieved.

'I thought I was never going to get rid of her,' he said, slumping into the nearest chair. 'The girl's like a leech once she's attached herself to someone!'

'You shouldn't be so irresistibly attractive to women,' remarked Cathryn, her eyes gleaming.

'Until now, I didn't think I was,' he replied drily. Then he glanced at his watch. 'Now that I've finally managed to shift her out of here, I've got a suggestion to put to you.'

Cathryn was instantly on her guard. 'What sort of suggestion?'

'Charles's flat is very comfortable, but I'm sick of staring at four walls all day. I want to get out of here.'

That didn't seem completely unreasonable to Cathryn. 'What do you want to do?' she asked. 'Go out for lunch? Or for a drive somewhere?'

Nicholas's green eyes glinted in the way that she was already beginning to distrust.

'I'd like to go for a drive,' he told her.

'Where to?'

'Cornwall,' he answered calmly.

Cathryn's eyebrows shot up. 'Cornwall?'

'I've a house down there,' he replied, to her

surprise. 'I want to go and stay there for a couple of days. I can't get there, though, unless someone drives me.' Then a light frown suddenly furrowed his forehead. 'I suppose you can drive?' he questioned her.

Cathryn considered lying to him, and telling him that she couldn't. She was sure that he would know she was lying, though; she had never been any good at it. Something in her face always gave her away.

'Yes, I can drive,' she said reluctantly. 'But I'm *not* volunteering to take you to Cornwall,' she added very firmly.

'Why not?' he asked reasonably. 'You'd like it there.'

'I like it here! Your brother's flat is very comfortable.'

'It's also stifling,' Nicholas growled. 'I look out of the window, and there's nothing to see except more houses. I step out of the door and there are city smells instead of fresh clean air.'

Cathryn looked at him rather sceptically. 'I didn't know you were a nature lover! Anyway, didn't you tell me that you had a flat in London? You can't hate it here so much if you choose to live here.'

'I need a base in town when I'm working. And yes, there are times when I like city life. But I've spent the last three months staring at the walls of a hospital room,' he muttered. 'And now I'm cooped up here, in Charles's flat. I'm beginning to feel so damned claustrophobic that it's driving me crazy!'

He slammed his fist down with some force on the arm of his chair, making Cathryn jump. There was a contained violence in this man that might have frightened her if it hadn't been obvious that most of the time he kept it well under control. It broke out in small bursts now and then, but never so fiercely that it seriously scared or worried her. It simply rattled her nerves, which made her feel even more irritable herself.

'I can understand why you want to get out of here, but I really don't think this is a good time to go shooting off to Cornwall,' she said, annoyed that he had even had the nerve to ask her.

'Give me a good reason why not,' he challenged her.

'Well—your brother expects you to stay *here*,' she said, aware that was a pretty feeble argument. 'He might ring up to check that you're all right. He'd get worried if he found you weren't here. Besides that, there are plenty of doctors on hand in London, if anything goes wrong—if you need them,' she finished, glancing at him slightly nervously since she knew that was beginning to tread on rather delicate ground.

Unexpectedly, though, Nicholas didn't take offence at her remarks. 'You mean, if I go completely ga-ga?' he said with some amusement. 'Are you expecting me to do that? What on earth has Charles been saying about me?'

'Not very much,' replied Cathryn, picking her words extremely carefully. 'He just said that you were still suffering—well, after-effects. That's hardly surprising. Getting blown up is a pretty traumatic thing to happen.'

'Yes, it is,' he agreed. 'But Charles seems to be under the impression that it'll take only a minor setback to send me completely out of my head. Delayed shock doesn't work like that.'

'Doesn't it?' Cathryn said doubtfully. 'I don't really know much about it.'

'I do,' came Nicholas's rather dry answer. 'During the course of my work, I've seen it in others plenty of times. Bad dreams, the shakes, spells when you get disorientated—and there are plenty of other symptoms you can get. There's not much you can do about them, either. You just have to sit it out, and wait until it works its way out of your system.'

'And not get too excited,' Cathryn reminded him, her eyebrows lifting gently.

'That, too,' he agreed with an unexpected grin. Then his expression changed again. 'I'm sure the doctors would approve of a change of scenery. So— will you drive me down to Cornwall?' he asked, looking at her directly.

'No, I won't,' Cathryn said decisively. 'I really think it would be better if you stayed here.'

Nicholas's good humour instantly vanished. 'I didn't ask you to make decisions about what was good for me. I'm quite capable of doing that for myself. All I wanted from you was a simple favour.'

'Simple?' Cathryn echoed indignantly. 'There's nothing particularly simple about a very long drive to the back of beyond!'

'Cornwall isn't completely beyond the bounds of civilisation. You can take the motorway for much of the journey. It's a fairly straightforward drive.'

'Straightforward or not, I'm not going,' Cathryn declared flatly. 'Your brother asked me to stay here with you, at this flat, and that's exactly what I intend to do.'

She had expected an outburst of temper, and perhaps even threats. Instead, though, Nicholas seemed to take her refusal very calmly. He levered himself to his feet and then looked down at her.

'If you won't drive me, then I'll just have to try and drive myself,' he said in a cool tone.

Her gaze immediately slid down to his injured leg. 'You can't!' she said in alarm. 'If you get into a car, you'll probably end up killing yourself. Or, worse still, you'll kill someone else!'

'That's a possibility,' Nicholas agreed smoothly. 'Of course, there's one way you can make sure neither of those things happen.'

'That's blackmail!' she accused. 'I don't like that.'

'Nor do I, usually. But I really do need to get away from here for a couple of days.'

There was a raw note in his voice now, that hadn't been there before. Cathryn glanced uneasily at him, and found his features were set in a dark, rigid pattern. She realised that he *did* need to get out of here. He was beginning to look like a caged animal that was growing quite desperate for freedom. But what would Sir Charles say if she went ahead with this? Would he hold her responsible if anything happened to his brother?

She gave a brief sigh. Was she really considering agreeing to this crazy plan? What was it about this man that could sometimes get to her?

'Like it or not, I feel responsible for you. That means I'd have to stay in Cornwall with you,' she said with a complete lack of enthusiasm. 'I couldn't just take you there and dump you.'

'I don't particularly want you hanging around, but if those are your terms for taking me then I suppose I'll have to go along with them.'

'You know perfectly well that I don't want to go at

all,' she retorted. 'Quite apart from anything else, I don't like the country. I'm a city girl. And I promised your brother——'

'Yes, I know,' interrupted Nicholas. 'To be honest I'm getting a little tired of hearing what you promised my brother. This whole set-up was absurd in the first place. I don't need a nursemaid, but I went along with it because I felt I owed my brother something for getting me out of that hospital.' He limped restlessly over to the window and stared out, like a prisoner searching for a glimpse of freedom. 'Well?' he said, turning back to face her. 'Will you take me?'

Cathryn definitely wanted to say no. She knew that if she refused, though, Nicholas was crazy enough to try and drive himself all that distance. And although it wouldn't really be her fault if anything happened, she would end up haunted by feelings of guilt.

'What if your brother rings?' she queried unhappily. 'He'll wonder where on earth we are.'

'I'll leave a message for him on the answerphone. Anyway, we'll only be away for a couple of days. A short break's all I need to get me back to some kind of sanity.'

Cathryn gave another sigh, only deeper this time. Somehow he was managing to make the whole thing sound so reasonable! He had a clever way with words—which was hardly surprising, considering his job.

'Are we leaving, then?' Nicholas challenged her softly. 'If we can get away during the next half-hour we should be there before dark.'

'I don't think this is a very good idea,' she warned

him. 'And I definitely don't like the way you're forcing me into it.'

'Stop arguing, and go and throw some clothes into a suitcase,' Nicholas told her.

Cathryn shook her head. If only there were some way she could get out of this! She couldn't seem to think of any, though. Not without declaring outright that she wasn't going, and letting Nicholas go careering off on his own.

Part of her wished that she could do just that. It was really inconvenient, having this strong sense of responsibility. She felt a great surge of resentment towards Nicholas Ellis, and wished she had never even heard of Sir Charles's brother. He was managing to turn her life upside-down, and she had only been here a couple of days so far!

With great reluctance, she went to her room and packed. When she trudged out into the hall with her case, she found Nicholas was already waiting for her.

'I wish you'd change your mind about this,' she said, frowning at him.

'I'm not going to do that, so let's get moving.'

'Whose car are we going to use?'

'My brother's,' replied Nicholas. 'It's in the garage round the back. Here are the keys.' He tossed them over to her.

Cathryn stared at him uneasily. 'I don't think we should use Sir Charles's car. Don't you have one of your own?'

'It's been garaged while I've been in hospital. By the time we've gone halfway across London to collect it, the best part of the day will be gone. We won't be able to reach Cornwall before dark.'

'I still don't like it,' she insisted. 'I mean, we don't

have permission to use it. And what about insurance?'

Nicholas began to look extremely impatient. 'Charles always insures everything very comprehensively, and that includes his cars. Incidentally, he's got three cars in all, and he rarely uses any of them. He goes everywhere by taxi. He certainly won't miss one of them for a couple of days.'

'That isn't the point,' she persisted.

'Then what is?' came his impatient growl. Nicholas looked as if he was getting very close to exploding, but that didn't deter Cathryn.

'Technically, it's theft,' she told him stubbornly.

'What do you want me to do?' came his caustic retort. 'Spend the rest of the day trying to get hold of my brother on the phone, so he can tell you himself that it's all right?'

'That would certainly make me feel a lot better about the whole thing,' Cathryn said, standing her ground even though the fierce blaze of Nicholas's eyes made her knees quiver.

He scowled irritably, and snatched up the phone. 'I'll make one try to get through to Charles. If I can't reach him, we'll simply take the car.'

'If you can't get hold of him, we'll cancel the trip until you *can* speak to him,' Cathryn said, her voice a lot firmer than her still shaking legs.

Nicholas flicked through the list of telephone numbers that his brother had left behind, and then dialled one of them. Cathryn wandered restlessly up and down while Nicholas spoke curtly to someone at the other end. Then she remembered the time difference between England and the States.

'It'll be very early in the morning over there,' she warned him.

'Fine,' said Nicholas grimly. 'We'll get Charles out of bed. And if he isn't at all pleased at having his sleep disturbed, remember that you're the one to blame.'

Cathryn indignantly began to deny it—after all, *she* wasn't the one who wanted to go haring off to Cornwall—but Nicholas didn't hear her. He was already speaking to someone at the other end.

'Yes, please keep ringing,' he said in a terse voice. 'I don't care if you wake him up.' There was another pause, rather longer this time, and then Nicholas said, 'Charles? Yes, I do know what time it is. I'm ringing to ask if we can use your car. Cathryn will be driving it, of course.' He listened to something that his brother said, and the taut line of his mouth relaxed a fraction. 'Yes, I *do* know that it wasn't necessary to call you at this time in the morning to ask you that, but I couldn't convince Cathryn of that fact. Do you want to speak to her?' Nicholas held the receiver out to Cathryn. 'My brother would like a word with you.'

Cathryn took it with some trepidation. 'Hello?' she said in a small voice.

'Cathryn, what on earth is this all about?' To her relief, Sir Charles sounded resigned rather than angry.

'Nicholas wants us to use your car, but I didn't like to take it without your permission,' she explained apologetically.

Sir Charles gave a sigh. 'Where does Nicholas want you to take him?'

'Er—Cornwall,' she told him.

'What the hell does he want to go there for?' asked Sir Charles in a baffled voice.

'Apparently, he's got a house there.'

'I didn't know that,' said Sir Charles, after a brief pause. 'But then, there's a great deal I've never really known or understood about my brother,' he said a trifle bitterly. 'What does he want to do? Stay at this house of his?'

Nicholas had moved out of earshot now, so Cathryn felt she could talk freely as long as she kept her voice low.

'Just for a couple of days. He says this flat is making him feel claustrophobic.'

'Nicholas never did like staying in the same place for too long,' commented Sir Charles. 'I suppose that's why he does the sort of job that he does. How do you feel about this trip, Cathryn?'

'Not too thrilled,' she admitted. 'But I'll stick with him, since I promised you that I would.'

'You're worth your weight in gold,' he said gratefully. 'Look, get the address of Nicholas's house and leave it in my diary on the desk. And when you get down there, see if there's a phone. If there is, give me a ring and leave the number. That way, I won't feel so out of touch with you.'

'OK, I'll do that,' she agreed.

'How are you coping in general?' he asked.

'About as well as I thought I would,' Cathryn said drily.

Sir Charles chuckled at the other end. 'As bad as that? I did warn you Nicholas wasn't an easy person to get along with.'

'To be honest, I don't think he really needs me

here,' she said. 'He's short-tempered, and he doesn't seem to be sleeping very well, but I don't think it's anything he can't handle on his own.'

'He may well stay fine,' agreed Sir Charles. 'Especially if he takes his medication regularly. But the specialist at the hospital did warn that there was a chance he could hit a really bad patch. And if that happens, he'll need someone around.'

'I don't know what I could actually do about it,' said Cathryn doubtfully.

'I don't expect you to do anything,' said Sir Charles. 'Just get him medical help as quickly as you can. The number of the specialist is in the phone book. Ring him, and he'll arrange to have Nicholas immediately readmitted to hospital.'

'But we're going to be in Cornwall,' Cathryn pointed out uneasily.

'I know,' said Sir Charles, the tone of his voice clearly telling her that he wasn't very pleased about that particular arrangement. 'Can't you talk him out of it?'

'I've tried,' she said ruefully.

'And you didn't get anywhere?' guessed Sir Charles with a great deal of resignation.

'With or without me, he intends to go.'

'Then take the number of the specialist with you,' Sir Charles told her. 'If anything happens, they'll arrange for a private ambulance to bring Nicholas back to London.'

Cathryn was beginning to get alarmed by all these rather elaborate arrangements. 'Is anything *likely* to happen?' she said. 'Is there something you're not telling me?'

'Certainly not,' Sir Charles assured her. 'Nicholas

will probably be fine. I just feel I need to take these precautions in case something out of the ordinary happens.'

'I think you worry too much about your brother,' Cathryn said bluntly. 'To be honest, he seems perfectly capable of looking after himself.'

There was a short pause from the other end. 'I don't really know what Nicholas is like nowadays,' Sir Charles said slowly, at last. 'But when he was younger—when we were closer—he always used to have a vulnerable side to him. Perhaps it isn't there any more. Maybe the nature of the work he does has knocked it out of him. But if he *does* still occasionally need someone to turn to, I want someone reliable to be there for him.'

'And I've been nominated as that person?' Cathryn said wryly.

'Only because I know that you won't let me down. There aren't many people I feel I can rely on completely, but you're one of them, Cathryn. And I really do appreciate everything that you're doing. I know that you can't be finding it at all easy.'

Cathryn didn't know quite what to say. And she certainly hoped she would never let him down, not after he had so openly declared his faith in her.

'You'd better be off now,' Sir Charles said, quietly breaking into the silence. 'It's a long drive down to Cornwall. Have a safe journey.'

Cathryn said goodbye, and then slowly put down the receiver. Sir Charles's feelings towards his younger brother certainly seemed to be very ambivalent. Something fairly dramatic must have happened in the past to have driven them so far apart. Sir Charles seemed to be taking the first steps towards healing that rift, though, and she wondered if Nicholas would ever unbend a little and allow himself to respond.

Nicholas must have heard her put down the phone because he reappeared in the doorway a few moments later. 'Ready to leave now?' he asked. 'Or are you trying to think up some other excuse for not going?'

'Sir Charles wants me to leave the address of your house in his diary,' Cathryn told him.

He scowled. 'Whatever for?'

'He wants to know where to get in touch with you. He *is* your brother,' Cathryn reminded him. 'It's not so odd that he wants to keep track of you.'

'It's odd that he's suddenly started to show all this concern,' Nicholas replied briefly. 'Anyway, the house doesn't have an address.'

Cathryn immediately looked at him with some suspicion. 'What do you mean, it doesn't have an address?'

'It's rather off the beaten track. It isn't on any officially named road, and it doesn't have a number.'

'What happens when they want to deliver letters or parcels to you?' she demanded, not sure that she believed this story he was spinning her.

'All my mail is addressed to my London flat.'

'Well—what if someone wants to get in touch with you urgently?'

'They can't,' he said briefly. 'That's the whole point of having a place like this. It's somewhere you can get away from everything and everyone.'

'If it hasn't got a number, has the house got a name?' she asked with a growing frown.

'It's called The Beach House.'

'How very original! I take it that it's on the coast?'

'Yes, it is,' agreed Nicholas, and the glimmerings of a smile began to show around his mouth. 'I'm not telling you anything else about it until we get there, though.'

'Oh, good,' she said, without the slightest trace of enthusiasm. 'I do like surprises.'

Nicholas picked up her case. 'Let's get going, or we won't get there before dark. You fetch the car while I bring out the bags.'

With a lot of reluctance—and quite a bit of trepidation about this entire trip—Cathryn made her way to the back of the house, and the garage where Sir Charles's car was kept. She unlocked the double doors and swung them open; then she stood and stared at the sleek two-seater that confronted her. Although it wasn't a new car, the paintwork gleamed, the chrome was positively dazzling, and it looked as if it were capable of passing almost anything else on four wheels.

Very nervously, Cathryn got in and settled herself behind the wheel. The very low mileage told her how little Sir Charles had driven this particular car, and she wondered why he had bought it in the first place. It certainly didn't seem to fit in with his image.

She switched on the ignition, and the engine purred throatily into life. With great care, she eased the car out of the garage, knowing that an incautious touch on the accelerator would send it shooting off far faster than she wanted it to go.

She drove round to the square and pulled up outside Sir Charles's flat. Nicholas was waiting for her, but, instead of loading their bags straight into the back, he simply stood and stared at the car for several seconds.

In the end, Cathryn got out. 'Not quite the car that you expected your rather staid brother to drive?' she said with a grin.

Nicholas didn't give her an answering smile.

'This isn't Charles's car,' he said slowly.

'But—it's got to be! I know I didn't go to the wrong garage. Anyway, I had the right keys for it,' Cathryn insisted.

His face remained grim. 'This car belonged to Charles's wife,' he stated flatly.

'His—his wife?' The smile vanished from Cathryn's mouth.

'Charles bought it for her just a few months before she died. It was a birthday present.'

'Some present,' murmured Cathryn under her breath. Then she uneasily touched the gleaming paintwork. 'Does that mean we can't use it?'

Nicholas shrugged. 'I shouldn't think so. Charles must have known this was the only car in his garage. If he hadn't wanted us to take it, he would have said so.' He picked up her case and his own canvas bag; then stowed them into the back. 'Can you handle a machine like this?' he questioned her.

'I can try.'

'Just keep your speed well down until you get the feel of it,' he advised.

Cathryn had every intention of doing just that. In fact, she drove so slowly at first that she could sense Nicholas becoming impatient. Once they joined the motorway, though, she became more bold and pressed her foot down a fraction. Immediately, the car responded with a burst of speed that left her slightly breathless. She eased it back to just under the speed limit, and let the car cruise along with its full potential held well in check.

'Do you mind if I ask you something?' she asked a few minutes later.

'About what?'

'It's about Sir Charles's wife,' she confessed.

Nicholas shot a quick glance at her. 'What do you want to know? Or is it just a general interest in the competition?'

'Competition?' she repeated, puzzled. 'Sir Charles's wife is dead!'

'Of course she is,' he agreed. 'And it's often a hell of a lot harder to compete against the dead than the living.'

'I'm not competing against anyone,' Cathryn retorted. 'I was just interested in knowing a little more about her. All I know is that she died five years ago. No one ever talks about her, though, or even mentions her name.'

'Her name was Helena,' said Nicholas, after a slight pause. 'She and Charles had been married just three years when she was killed in a car crash.'

'Was she driving?' asked Cathryn, after a moment's silence.

'Yes, she was. And she was alone in the car. Not this car, of course,' Nicholas added. 'It was one of Charles's other cars.'

'What caused the accident?'

'No one ever knew for sure. The weather was good and the road surface quite dry. She did have well over the legal amount of alcohol in her blood, though. The car ran straight off the road and wrapped itself around a tree. Helena was killed instantly.'

'Your brother must have taken it very hard,' she said softly.

'He was devastated,' Nicholas said a little roughly. 'He adored that woman. From the day he met her, there was never anyone else for him. There never will be. In his eyes, she was absolutely perfect, and the only one he ever wanted. He wouldn't even accept that she had been drinking before the accident. Right to this day, he keeps insisting that there must have been some mistake made during the tests.'

Cathryn shook her head. 'That doesn't sound at all like Sir Charles.'

'Everyone has their blind spot,' replied Nicholas. 'And Helena was his. That's why you're never going to get anywhere with my brother,' he told her, his voice becoming a little grimmer. 'Helena's still got her dead fingers wrapped firmly around his heart.'

Cathryn shivered a little at his words. They didn't conjure up a very nice picture. 'I don't *want* to get anywhere with your brother,' she replied in a low voice. 'I enjoy working for him, but I'm not interested in him personally—and I'm certainly not chasing him because of his money.'

Nicholas looked fairly sceptical. 'If you're telling the truth, that's just as well, because you don't have a hope in hell of catching him. He'll go to his grave still loving Helena. He was deliberately blind to her faults, and refused to let anyone disillusion him about her.'

'Disillusion him?' repeated Cathryn, drawing her brows together. 'What do you mean?'

'Just that Helena wasn't quite the person that Charles imagined her to be.'

'In what way?'

'You do like to dig into all our dark family secrets, don't you?' Nicholas remarked.

She flushed heavily. 'No one's forcing you to tell me about them,' she said defensively.

'No, I suppose not,' he said with a shrug. 'And perhaps it doesn't really matter quite so much after all this time. Have you ever seen a photograph of Helena?' he asked, rather unexpectedly.

'Yes, of course. Sir Charles keeps a photo of her on his desk.'

'What do you think of her?'

'That she wasn't exactly beautiful,' said Cathryn slowly. 'She was somehow too delicate-looking—those frail little bones, the big, childlike eyes, that fluffy pale hair. She was the type that men often go for, though. They'd want to look after her, protect her, I should think. She gave the impression of not being able to survive without a strong arm to lean on.'

'You *are* perceptive,' Nicholas said, with some surprise. 'That was precisely what Helena was like. But she was mentally frail, as well as physically. She was either way up or way down. And she had a lot of weaknesses.'

Cathryn wondered what those weaknesses were, but didn't quite have the nerve to ask.

'She was genuinely in love with my brother, though,' Nicholas went on. 'And she lived in dread of letting him down or in some way disappointing him. But at the same time she seemed to have the knack of getting into serious trouble. And she could never cope with it herself. She would always look round for someone to bail her out. Never Charles, though. Charles was never allowed to know about any of her mistakes. She couldn't have borne it if his image of her had been shattered. And perhaps Charles couldn't have borne it, either,' he remarked to himself in a soft tone.

'It sounds like a rather odd relationship to me,' Cathryn commented.

'Perhaps it was, but it seemed to work—up to a point.'

Cathryn was dying to ask what point that was, but knew that she had already probed too far into something that was really none of her business. With reluctance, she dropped the subject and concentrated instead on her driving.

After an hour on the motorway, she realised it was well past lunchtime and she was starving. Nicholas was reluctant to stop, but Cathryn simply ignored his arguments, steered the car into the next service area and then headed towards the restaurant. There were certain advantages in being the driver, and she had decided to make the most of them. Advantages were few and far between when Nicholas Ellis was around!

After they had eaten, it was back on to the motorway again. Cathryn enjoyed driving, and especially this particular car. It responded to the lightest touch on the wheel, and would have roared off at a quite illegal speed if she had given it half a chance. Its only drawback was that it had originally belonged to Sir Charles's wife, which made her feel faintly uneasy, as if there was the shadow of a ghost riding in the car with them. She tried hard not to think of it, and concentrated instead on controlling the powerful machine.

During the hours of the afternoon, they headed on towards the West Country, following the motorway and then main trunk roads for most of the way. Since it was late autumn there was very little tourist traffic, and none of the hold-ups that snarled up the roads in the summer. They made another short stop well into the afternoon, but not for long. By this time, Cathryn was as anxious as Nicholas to reach their destination before night set in. Driving this car in the dark on unknown roads would be no joke.

Eventually Nicholas directed her along a couple of minor roads, and she could sense that they were nearing the coast. There was a tang in the air; a hint of saltiness that grew stronger as they neared the still invisible sea.

The road twisted and turned, winding through countryside that was already beginning to look a little desolate as the last of the summer colours faded. Then it began to descend and Cathryn could see the sea. She could also see houses, some of grey stone and some brightly painted, all of them tumbling towards a small harbour that sheltered maybe a couple of dozen boats.

She had to admit that it was very picturesque. 'Is one of those houses yours?' she asked Nicholas, deciding that a couple of days here might not be so bad, after all.

'Not exactly,' he replied. 'Pull up the car for a moment.'

She stopped by the side of the road, just before it entered the village. Then she found Nicholas was pointing out to sea.

'See that?' he said.

She realised he was directing her attention to a small island about a mile away.

'Of course,' she replied. 'What about it?'

'*That's* where my house is,' replied Nicholas.

CHAPTER FIVE

CATHRYN thought he was joking. Before this, she hadn't credited Nicholas with much of a sense of humour, but obviously he had one. Then she looked at his face, and found that he looked completely serious.

'You're pulling my leg,' she said uneasily. 'Right?'

He frowned. 'Pulling your leg about what?'

'About your house being on that island, of course!'

His frown deepened. 'Why would I joke about it?'

Cathryn didn't at all like the way this was going. 'How can you live on an island?' she challenged him. 'It—it just isn't practical,' she finished rather lamely.

'No, it isn't,' Nicholas agreed regretfully. 'That's one reason why I don't spend as much time there as I'd like to.'

But Cathryn still didn't quite believe that this wasn't an elaborate hoax.

'You'll be telling me next that you own the island!'

Nicholas shook his head. 'It's owned by a friend of mine. I couldn't possibly afford to buy it. I can only just afford the lease on the house. Paying for that, and keeping my flat going in London, just about stretches my finances to their limit.'

It was slowly beginning to dawn on Cathryn that all of this was for real, and he really expected her to spend the next couple of days stuck on an isolated little island.

'How many other people live there?' she asked. If

it turned out to have a fairly healthy population, then she supposed she might just manage to cope with this totally unexpected turn of events.

Nicholas shrugged. 'At this time of the year, we'll probably be the only ones there.'

'The only ones?' squeaked Cathryn.

'It's a very small island, and it only has three houses,' Nicholas told her, apparently undisturbed by her reaction. 'One belongs to my friend, Hamish Ferguson, who owns the island, the second one is used by Hamish's brother and his family, and the third house Hamish leases to me.'

But Cathryn had already heard more than enough. 'I'm not staying on a totally deserted island,' she said with great firmness. 'And there's absolutely nothing you can say that will make me change my mind!'

'I'm not even going to try,' Nicholas answered, to her complete surprise.

She blinked at him. 'You're not?'

'Why bother?' he said with a shrug. 'The solution's very simple. I'll head over to the island, and you can drive back to London.'

Cathryn stared at him in sudden comprehension. 'This is what you had in mind all along, wasn't it?' she accused. 'You knew it would be a good way to get rid of me. That's why you didn't tell me in London that your house was stuck on some wretched island!'

'My motives are rarely that complicated,' he drawled. 'The reason I didn't tell you about the island was that I knew you'd refuse to bring me here.'

Cathryn found herself caught in a complete dilemma. There was no way she wanted to set foot on that island. How could she let Nicholas go there by himself, though? Especially after she had promised Sir Charles only this morning that she would stick with him?

'If I go back to London, you'd really stay here by yourself?' she said slowly.

Nicholas didn't hesitate for one moment. 'Of course.'

'But that's crazy!' she said angrily. 'What if something happened to you on that island? Who'd be around to help you?'

'No one,' he said calmly. 'As usual, I'd have to look after myself.'

'You sound so blasé about the whole thing!' she snapped back at him. 'Don't you have any sense of responsibility?'

A glow of irritation finally began to show in Nicholas's own eyes. 'Yes, I have, but you and my brother seem determined to stop me from exercising it! You're watching over me and mollycoddling me as if I were a child, and it's driving me crazy. Charles still seems to think of me as the young brother he had to look out for and protect when we were kids, and he's got you thinking along the same lines. Well, let me tell you something—I don't *need* that kind of concern any more. Over the last few years I've been in dozens of hair-raising situations, and I've always looked out for myself and got myself out of them. All right, the last three months have been rough, but I've got through them, and I'm not about to crack up. If I were, I'd have done it by now. I'll admit I'm grateful to Charles for getting me out of that hospital, and I've gone along with all this brotherly concern because, for some reason, he seemed to need to show it. But I've had enough! From now on, I'm taking charge of my own life again, and doing exactly what *I* want to do. You can either tag along, or you can go back to London and tell Charles that you've resigned as nursemaid!'

It was the longest speech she had ever heard him make—and perhaps the most honest. For once, he was being completely straight with her, telling her exactly how he felt. And to her surprise she found herself sympathising with him.

'I suppose it is pretty frustrating, having other people trying to run your life for you,' she admitted. 'But at least it shows that your brother does care for you. I know there's been a lot of bad feeling between the two of you, but perhaps this is his way of telling you that he's trying to bridge that gap and make things right again.'

'Maybe,' growled Nicholas. 'I don't really know what motivates my brother any more.'

'Then perhaps this is a good time to find out,' Cathryn suggested.

His green gaze blazed at her. 'Don't lecture me! I can sort out my own life and my own problems. All I want to know right now is whether you're going back to London, or hanging around to annoy me for a while longer.'

Cathryn sighed. 'I suppose I'm going to annoy you by hanging around. I think you're right, you *don't* need a nursemaid any more. But a promise is a promise. I can't break it.'

'It must be very inconvenient, having such strong moral scruples.'

Cathryn glared at him. Was he mocking her? He had already turned away, though, and she couldn't see his face clearly.

'Let's get going,' he instructed curtly. 'I want to reach the island before nightfall. Follow the road down to the harbour.'

She started up the car again, and at the same time told herself that she must be mad. There was no other description for someone who agreed to spend a couple of days on a deserted island with Nicholas Ellis!

When they reached the harbour, Nicholas pointed out an empty area where she could park the car. As soon as she had switched off the engine he levered himself out and began to remove their bags.

Cathryn also got out and stretched her tired limbs. Then she looked around at the picturesque little village, with its steep, narrow streets, the tiny harbour which sheltered the boats, and the houses which huddled up close to each other against the background of hills.

'This place must be crawling with tourists in the summer,' she commented.

'It's rather off the beaten track, so it doesn't suffer as much as a lot of the other villages along this coast,' commented Nicholas as he lifted out the last bag. 'Here, you can carry your own suitcase,' he added.

'Ever heard of gallantry?' she muttered, as she went to pick it up. Then she immediately flushed. She had momentarily forgotten about his bad leg.

Nicholas didn't seem bothered by her thoughtless remark, though. 'There's no need to go bright red,' he told her. 'I'm not embarrassed in any way by my injury, so why should you be? And it'll heal itself in time. Then I'll be as gallant as you want me to be,' he finished with a sly grin.

Cathryn frowned crossly. He was so good at making her feel off balance!

She was still feeling distinctly out of sorts as she followed him towards the harbour. Not even the tranquil beauty of her surroundings could quite lift her edgy mood.

The tide was fully in, and she could hear it slapping softly against the stone walls. It should have been a soothing sound, and yet somehow it just grated on her nerves. Nicholas had stopped now, standing beside steep stone steps that led down to half a dozen boats moored alongside the jetty. Cathryn took one look at their wet, slippery surface, and then shifted her gaze back to Nicholas.

'You can't go down there,' she said baldly. 'You'll break your neck!'

'Of course I won't,' he replied calmly.

'Then I'll break *my* neck—which is far worse, as far as I'm concerned!'

'No one's going to break anything,' he said with unexpected patience. 'Just take it slow and easy, and we'll make it without any problems.'

Almost before he had finished speaking, he had begun to tackle the steps. Moving carefully, and occasionally steadying himself with his stick, he soon reached the foot of the steps.

'Your turn now,' he said with a challenging grin.

Cathryn scowled, and then set about tackling the steps. She finally made it safely to the bottom, and Nicholas pointed to a tiny cabin cruiser moored just a short way along the jetty. 'Sling your case in there, and then scramble in. I'll untie the mooring ropes.'

'It looks awfully small,' Cathryn commented nervously.

Nicholas raised his dark eyebrows. 'What were you expecting? A luxury yacht?'

'No, but—isn't there something bigger we could use?'

'Afraid not. Anyway, this is perfectly adequate. It's only a short hop to the island.'

It didn't look like a short hop to Cathryn! And she would definitely have felt a lot safer in a boat that was large and solid, rather than in this flimsy little cabin cruiser.

'The sea's like a mill-pond today,' added Nicholas, tossing his own bag into the boat, and then manoeuvring himself in with rather more care.

Cathryn stared gloomily at the light swell of the sea and decided that it didn't look like any mill-pond *she* had ever seen.

You've still got time to back out, she reminded herself. Just tell Nicholas you've changed your mind—he'll be only too pleased to get you off this boat and send you on your way back to London!

Something kept her sitting exactly where she was, though, gripping very tightly on to the side of the boat as Nicholas started up the engine, and then steered the boat out of the harbour and towards the open sea.

Now that they were actually on the water, the island did, in fact, look fairly close.

'I suppose if anything went drastically wrong— you know, the boat sank or something—we could always swim back to the mainland?' she said nervously.

'Only if you want to risk getting swept out to sea,' replied Nicholas. 'Strong currents run between the

island and the mainland. Only a real fool—or someone extremely brave—would tackle that stretch of
water.'

Cathryn quickly decided that she was neither, and
abandoned all thoughts of swimming to safety if
things took a turn for the worse.

They were nearing the island now, and she could
see that it stuck out of the water like an elongated
hump. The shoreline looked rocky and treacherous,
and Cathryn bit her lip in renewed trepidation.

'Er—I suppose there is a safe landing-spot?' she
said edgily.

'There's a tiny patch of beach and a jetty—landing's no problem in fine weather like this.'

Cathryn was about to ask what happened in not-
so-fine weather, but then decided that she didn't
really want to know.

They were close enough now for her to see more
details. There were trees on this side of the island,
which surprised her because she had thought that all
offshore islands were windswept and bleak. And she
could see two houses, one near the jetty, which she
could now pick out, and another at the far end of the
island.

'Where's the third house?' she asked. 'You did say
there were three, didn't you?'

'Yes. The third house belongs to Hamish. It's on
the far side of the island. The house near the jetty is
mine.'

'The island's a lot more green than I thought it
would be.'

Nicholas gave an amused smile. 'What were you
expecting? Bare, sea-washed rock?'

'No, of course not,' she said crossly. 'I just didn't expect it to have so many trees.'

'Most offshore islands don't, but this one has a warm current washing past it, so the climate's a lot milder than you'd expect. In fact, the previous owner used to grow early daffodils commercially. Hamish doesn't bother because there's a great deal of work involved and very little profit margin, but the daffodils still keep coming up every year. In late winter and early spring, the island's a blaze of colour. I always try to get down here at that time, if I can.'

Cathryn looked at him in surprise. 'You don't strike me as a daffodil person!'

'I can appreciate beauty as well as the next man,' he replied, and this time his gaze lingered on her a little longer than seemed strictly necessary.

Suddenly confused for some reason that she couldn't quite fathom, Cathryn forced her own gaze to the island. 'We're getting very close,' she observed.

'Just a few more minutes, and you'll be back on dry land.'

'I just wish it were the mainland,' she said darkly.

'A couple of days here and you'll love it,' Nicholas told her.

Cathryn merely looked sceptical. 'I doubt it. I'm a city girl, remember?'

'I've heard other people say the same thing, but they change their mind once they get here.'

Cathryn thought that it would take a lot to change *her* mind. She didn't argue with him any more, though, because they were getting very close to the jetty and she didn't want to distract him in any way.

It seemed a rather tricky operation to her, manoeuvring the small boat alongside it. She didn't want anything to go wrong and then have Nicholas blame her for it!

Getting out of the boat proved much harder than getting in. Cathryn finally managed it, although rather ungracefully, and was annoyed to find that Nicholas managed it better than she did, even with a bad leg.

He secured the boat, and then turned to her. 'We'd better get straight up to the house. It'll be growing dark soon.'

In fact, the light was already fading, and there was a distinct autumn chill in the air. The path up to the house was fairly steep and uneven, and the house itself had whitewashed walls and a sharply sloping slate roof. Behind it rose the main hump of the island, and a wide band of trees that acted as a windbreak.

Nicholas seemed to be tackling the path without too much difficulty, expertly using his stick to help keep his balance, and Cathryn looked at him with some suspicion.

'For someone who could hardly hobble from room to room a couple of days ago, you're doing remarkably well!'

He merely grinned. 'It's all this sea air. It's already having a beneficial effect on me.'

'In more ways than one,' Cathryn remarked. 'You're smiling a lot more. That must be the third grin in the last hour. That's got to be a record!'

'I'm really a very nice guy,' he told her. 'It's just that you haven't had a chance to find that out yet.'

'Mm,' said Cathryn sceptically. 'All I can say is that

you've been working awfully hard to keep all that niceness hidden!'

A couple of minutes later they reached the front door of the house. Nicholas unlocked it and walked inside. Cathryn followed him, and clicked down the light switch as the failing light made it quite dark inside.

Nothing happened, and she felt a twinge of panic. 'What's wrong?' she said sharply. 'Why won't the lights come on?'

Nicholas turned and looked at her, his face a pale blur in the gloom.

'Where do you suppose the electricity's coming from?' he asked.

She blinked. 'You mean, there isn't any?'

'We'd hardly be connected up to the national grid out here,' he pointed out.

'I suppose not,' she muttered, realising that she was being rather stupid. 'What do we do, then? Grope around in the dark?'

Even with the lack of light, she could see the gleam in his eyes. 'What a very nice thought,' he murmured. 'Right now, I feel exactly like a spot of groping.'

'Cut that out,' she said at once. 'I'm not in the mood for it. Go and find some candles, or whatever it is you use around here for light.'

'What we use is a generator,' he informed her, the amusement back in his voice now. 'Once I've got it going, you can have all the light you want.'

He limped through a door at the back, and seemed to be gone for a very long time. Cathryn stood there in the gathering darkness and felt her knees gently quiver. She didn't like this place. She had been here less than half an hour, but she definitely didn't like it!

A short while later, the light suddenly came on, and she gave a sigh of relief. Her nerves stopped twitching quite so badly, and she began to take a good look around the room.

It was comfortably, if a little sparsely, furnished, and from the windows you could see over to the mainland, which made her feel very slightly better. At least she could *see* civilisation, even if it did seem rather out of reach at the moment.

Nicholas came back a couple of minutes later and subsided into the nearest chair.

'I need to rest,' he announced. 'If you want to take a look around, you'll have to do it without me. Not that there's much to see. There are two bedrooms and a small bathroom upstairs, two rooms and the kitchen downstairs.'

Cathryn saw that he did indeed look very tired, and realised that this journey must have been quite a strain for him. After all, he had only been out of the hospital for a few days.

'I'll go upstairs and unpack,' she told him. 'Which room is mine?'

'The one on the left at the top of the stairs.'

She picked up her suitcase and trudged up to her room, which turned out to contain a bed, a chest of drawers, and virtually nothing else.

'Not exactly home from home,' she murmured, remembering the luxury of Sir Charles's flat with more than a twinge of regret. She shovelled her clothes into the drawers, and then went along to the bathroom to see if she could find some sheets and blankets for the bed. She was relieved to find the linen cupboard stocked with everything she needed. She made up her bed, and then went back downstairs.

She found that Nicholas had fallen asleep in the chair. It wasn't a light doze, either. He was deeply asleep.

Cathryn was about to walk out again, leaving him to sleep on undisturbed, but at the last moment she paused, turned back, and then stared at him. This was the first time she had had a chance to study him like this, and she found herself curiously eager to take advantage of it.

The marks of his injuries and all those weeks in hospital were printed quite clearly on his face. There were dark shadows under his eyes, his skin had an unhealthy pallor, and his features looked gaunt. But there wasn't any aura of weakness around this man. Despite all Sir Charles's warnings about possible relapses, Nicholas gave the impression of being very much in charge of himself.

Cathryn's gaze slid down until it rested on the scars that marked his hands and wrists. She found herself wondering what other scars he had, hidden by his clothes and his thick dark hair. Then there were the mental scars—the ones that nobody would ever be able to see, unless Nicholas Ellis gave express permission. He was a man who zealously guarded his privacy.

Then Nicholas opened one eye. 'Finished your inspection?' he enquired. Cathryn had taken an involuntary step back as soon as she had seen the movement of his eye.

'I thought you were asleep!' she said indignantly,

annoyed by the way that her pulses had suddenly begun to pound.

'I was,' he agreed, opening his other eye so that the full force of his green gaze blazed up at her. 'But I sleep very lightly. Perhaps you'd better remember that, in future.'

'I wasn't *interested* in you,' Cathryn denied at once. 'I was just—just——'

'Just staring at me,' he finished for her. Fresh curiosity showed on his face. 'Why?'

'No reason at all!' she snapped back at him. A scowl crossed her own features. 'I'm hungry,' she announced, absolutely determined to change the subject. 'I'm going to get something to eat. Do you want anything?' she added, forcing herself to make the offer out of sheer politeness. Although she didn't know *why* she was being polite, when Nicholas so rarely bothered with the common courtesies.

'I'll get something later on,' he said. He was already yawning again, and looked as if he was planning on going straight back to sleep as soon as she had left the room.

Cathryn walked towards the doorway, but then stopped again. 'I suppose there *is* something to eat?' she enquired. 'I mean, we didn't bring any food with us.'

'There's no fresh food,' agreed Nicholas. 'I'll take the boat over in the morning and raid the local store. There are plenty of tins, though. I always keep in a good stock in case the weather suddenly turns bad. Sometimes you can't get over to the mainland for days, even weeks. Eating out of tins gets a bit monotonous, but at least it means you don't actually starve.'

But Cathryn was no longer listening. Her eyes had shot wide open when he had made that remark about being cut off for days.

'Is it something that happens often?' she questioned him sharply. 'Being cut off, I mean?'

Nicholas shrugged, and didn't seem nearly as concerned as she was. 'It depends on the time of year. And the prevailing weather conditions. The weather's pretty good right now, and the forecast doesn't give for any dramatic changes in the next couple of days. There shouldn't be any problems.'

Cathryn slowly relaxed again. 'I'll get some supper, then. And after that I think I'll have an early night. It's been quite a day,' she added meaningfully. 'By the way, if I want something hot, how do I go about it? I mean, are you on a real back-to-nature kick here? Heating things up over wood fires, and all that?'

He grinned back at her. 'I like it here because it's peaceful and quiet, not because it's primitive. There's a small electric stove that works off the generator.'

'Thank heavens for that!' she said with some relief. Then she finally left the room and made her way to the kitchen.

Like the rest of the house, it wasn't exactly stuffed with gadgets and furnishings, but it seemed to have all the basic equipment. Cathryn sorted through the cupboards, trying to find out where everything was kept, and finally opened the door of the larder. As Nicholas had promised, it was well stocked with tins and any other kinds of food that would keep. Cathryn finally decided to settle for some soup. It wasn't very exciting, but it would keep her going until the morning, when Nicholas would get in some fresh stuff.

It didn't take her long to finish her meal. And, as she sat in the kitchen on her own, it struck her how very *quiet* it was here. Not a sound, except for the murmur of the sea. Cathryn found it quite unsettling. She was used to the busy roar of traffic, and the sound of distant voices and music. Silence was all very well, and there were times in her hectic work schedule when she sometimes craved it, but this was really taking it just a little too far!

She decided to go up to bed before this place really started to get to her. Perhaps she would cope with it a little better in the morning, when the sun was shining and she could see the mainland again. Right now, she felt as if she was stuck in the middle of nowhere!

She reached the foot of the stairs just as Nicholas ambled out of the lounge. For some reason, the sight of him immediately unsettled Cathryn. Flustered for no good reason that she could think of, she launched straight into what she thought would be a safe topic of conversation.

'I'm rather worried about your brother's car. Is it safe to leave it where we did, by the harbour?'

'As safe as it'll be anywhere.'

'But what if it's vandalised? Or stolen? I mean, we're responsible for it. If we hadn't borrowed it, it would still be stored safely away in the garage in London.'

'Garages can be broken into,' Nicholas pointed out. 'Especially in London. There's very little vandalism and theft around here, particularly out of season.'

'You don't seem very concerned about it,' Cathryn retorted in a rather annoyed voice.

'Perhaps I just don't set too much store by material possessions,' Nicholas suggested.

She glanced around the sparsely furnished house. 'Maybe that's because you don't have too many of them!'

To her surprise, he didn't take offence. 'You could be right,' he agreed. Then he yawned, as if he wasn't really interested in this conversation. 'Are you going up to bed?' he asked.

She was about to say yes, when she suddenly stopped. There was a brightness in Nicholas's eyes that she couldn't remember seeing before. She didn't know if it was a flicker of amusement—or something else.

Her wariness must have showed on her face, because the corners of his mouth lifted gently.

'Am I making you nervous, Cathryn?' he enquired gently.

'Of course not!' she snapped back instantly. 'What a perfectly ridiculous thing to say!'

'You've certainly never seemed scared of me before,' he agreed. 'But then, this is the first time we've been alone like this.'

'We were alone at Sir Charles's flat,' she pointed out stiffly. 'At least, until Mandy showed up,' she added, with more than a touch of sarcasm.

'It wasn't quite the same, though, was it?' mused Nicholas. 'There were people in the flats above, and in the other houses all around us.'

'I wouldn't have come here with you if I'd been in the least scared of you,' she said, in what she hoped was a very firm voice.

'No, I suppose not.' He studied her thoughtfully. 'Why *did* you come, Cathryn?'

But she had had enough of this interrogation. 'You know perfectly well it was because of my promise to your brother!'

'Oh, yes—the famous promise.' Somehow, he made it sound like a very lame excuse for being here, and Cathryn grew more angry.

'You don't think I came because of *you*?' she demanded.

'That really would be a very egotistical assumption to make,' he agreed. And yet his tone of voice clearly told her that he was actually considering it.

'Since we're on the subject, why did you let me stay?' she challenged him. 'All right, you needed me to drive you down here. You could have sent me straight back to London, though. After all, you didn't *want* me hanging around all the time, did you?'

'I certainly didn't think so at the time,' replied Nicholas. 'Why did I let you stay?' His tone had become thoughtful now. 'I'm rather beginning to wonder that myself.'

As they faced each other, Cathryn slightly pink and hot now while Nicholas remained outwardly cool, there seemed to be a subtle change in the atomosphere between them. At first, Cathryn thought she was imagining it. There had been no sudden crackle in the air, no visible sign of change. It was more a lessening of tension—the relaxation of taut muscles and the dissolving of the last traces of bad temper.

Nicholas seemed as surprised by it as she was. He took a step forward, paused, and then looked at her long and hard before taking yet another step.

Cathryn was certain that she should move, and yet she didn't. Nor could she seem to look away from

Nicholas's face, which suddenly seemed to have taken on a new aspect. His features were like those of an old friend, whom she had known all her life. Except she was quite certain that Nicholas required a great deal more than friendship from his women. . .

She cleared her throat with fresh nervousness. 'I—er—I think it's time I went up to bed.'

'Yes—bed,' he repeated softly.

A warning shiver ran over her skin. Rather belatedly, she realised she could easily get into something she would find hard to handle.

'There's not much point in thinking along those lines,' she advised him crisply. 'Remember what the doctors told you. You've got to live like a monk for the next three or four weeks!'

'I haven't forgotten,' he said regretfully. The gleam briefly showed in his eyes again. 'I suppose a very brief goodnight kiss wouldn't be too exciting.'

'It wouldn't excite *me*,' Cathryn retorted at once. 'And I really don't think it's necessary.'

'No, not necessary,' he agreed. 'Just rather pleasant.' He moved closer. 'What do you think, Cathryn?'

'I think you're in a very odd mood tonight!'

'You could be right.' There was a flash of green as the light shone directly in his eyes. Too late, Cathryn realised it was because he was already bending his head towards her.

A moment later, his lips were over hers, warm and firm. Their pressure wasn't insistent or demanding; instead, they moved gently, as if savouring these few moments of warm pleasure. Then, although she hadn't expected it, he released her.

'Nice—but frustrating,' he said drily.

More off balance than she cared to admit, Cathryn

glared at him. 'Then don't try it again!' she snapped back at him.

'Because you didn't like it?' Nicholas enquired with interest. 'Or because you liked it a lot better than you ever expected?' he said more huskily.

Cathryn didn't answer because she was suddenly afraid that she wouldn't be able to tell a very convincing lie. Instead, she swung round and retreated with dignity up the stairs, hoping that he would draw his own conclusions from the deliberate stiffness of her back.

Once in her own room, though, she sat on the edge of the bed and let her eyebrows shoot up sky-high in pure surprise. Nicholas was right, she *hadn't* expected to like it. Only she had! She had liked it a lot.

She was never going to let him know that, of course. And she definitely wasn't going to let it happen again! Not only did she not trust Nicholas, but for the first time in a very long while Cathryn was no longer quite so certain that she trusted herself.

CHAPTER SIX

THE water that came out of the tap in the bathroom was only lukewarm, but Cathryn supposed she ought to be grateful that it wasn't completely stone-cold. She quickly washed, and wished that Nicholas had bought a house with a few more amenities—and in a less God-forsaken spot. On the other hand, he might well be needing a few cold baths before his weeks of enforced celibacy were up!

She scuttled back to the bedroom, wincing a little as her feet hit the chilly floor. When she climbed into bed, it was as cold as everything else around here seemed to be. The sheets were icy against her skin, and Cathryn wished she had brought thick wincey-ette pyjamas instead of a cotton nightshirt.

It was ages before she got to sleep. She lay there and shivered for what seemed like half the night, partly because she was cold and partly because this place seemed really spooky once it had got dark.

She eventually managed to doze off, and when she opened her eyes again she was relieved to find it was full daylight. In bright sunshine, things never seemed quite so bad.

She washed and dressed, and then made her way cautiously downstairs. Was Nicholas already up? she wondered. The house seemed completely silent, and she hoped that meant he was still in bed. After that unexpectedly disturbing kiss last night, she wasn't in any hurry to face him again!

The sun might have been shining, but it didn't seem to be warming up the interior of the house. A chill seemed to lie over all the rooms, and she wished she had brought warmer clothes with her. What was it Nicholas had said about this island having a mild climate? Well, right now, it didn't feel very mild to her!

The two downstairs rooms were empty, and so was the kitchen. Cathryn sighed with relief. Nicholas must be sleeping late. Then she noticed the note propped up on the kitchen table.

'Gone to fetch provisions. Back later. Be good while I'm away! Nicholas.'

Cathryn stared at it. He had *gone*? He had left her completely alone on this wretched island?

She ran to the door, flung it open, and stared down towards the jetty. The boat wasn't there. He *had* gone.

She had completely forgotten that she hadn't wanted to see him. Right now, all she could think about was that she was stuck on this wretched piece of rock, completely cut off from the rest of the world. She had never felt so totally alone in her entire life!

'I wish I'd never come here,' she muttered shakily under her breath. 'I wish I'd never heard of Nicholas Ellis!'

She went back to the kitchen and made herself some coffee, but then couldn't manage to drink it. Usually, she didn't mind her own company, but this was a very different sort of loneliness. She knew she couldn't pick up the phone and chat to someone; couldn't walk out of the door and meet other people. If she wanted a conversation, it would have to be with a seagull!

'No one in their right mind would want to spend any time in a place like this,' she told herself edgily. 'It's like living in the back of nowhere!'

She knew she was exaggerating slightly. After all, she could see the mainland quite clearly. She *felt* so cut-off, though. That narrow strip of water might as well have been a hundred miles wide. She couldn't swim it; there wasn't even a boat that would take her across it, not until Nicholas got back. Her sense of isolation grew, and so did her temper. How dared he leave her on her own like this? He must have known how very scared it would make her feel.

It seemed like half a lifetime before she finally spotted the small boat chugging its way back towards the island. She ran down to meet it, and was yelling at Nicholas even before he had begun to get out.

'Why did you go off like that? You didn't even warn me you were going! Only a real rat would do something like that!'

Nicholas glanced up at her in surprise, obviously having no idea what she was ranting on about. 'What's the problem?' he asked.

'The problem?' she screeched right back at him. 'The problem is that I've been stuck here on this island on my own, and I *hate* it. I didn't even know when you were coming back. Or *if* you were coming back.'

Nicholas levered himself out of the boat and limped over to her. 'Do you really think I'd just clear off and leave you here?' he asked a little tautly.

'I don't know what you'd do!' she yelled. 'For all I know, you might think it was really funny to do something like that!'

His fingers gripped her arm. 'I don't have that kind

of a sense of humour,' he told her sharply. Then he shook her lightly. 'Get this into some sort of proportion, Cathryn. I didn't tell you I was going because you were fast asleep. I didn't want to disturb you. I left you a note, though, and you knew damned well I'd be coming back. Didn't you?' he persisted giving her another shake.

'I suppose so,' she muttered.

Nicholas's grip on her arm became less intense. 'Then why this big scene?' His finger hooked itself under her chin and pulled her face towards him, so he could stare directly down at her. 'Were you really that scared?' he said, his brows drawing together in a deep frown.

Cathryn was beginning to feel rather silly. 'I must have been, mustn't I?' she said, a faintly sulky note entering her voice now.

He still looked sceptical. 'I thought you were the girl who could cope with everything. According to Charles, absolutely nothing ever throws you.'

'Which just goes to show that your brother doesn't know everything about me!' she retorted.

'He also said that you never lose your temper,' remarked Nicholas. 'He wasn't quite right about that, either.'

'I never did—until you came along!'

'Life must have been very boring before you met me,' commented Nicholas. Then, before she could throw a furious answer back at him, he gestured towards the boxes in the boat. 'Shall we take this lot up to the house?'

'You've managed to get it this far. *You* carry it up. I'm going to have some breakfast.'

With that, she marched up to the house, not once

looking round to see if Nicholas was having any problems hauling the boxes of food up the steep slope.

Once back in the kitchen, she put the kettle on to boil, to make some fresh coffee. Just as it was boiling, Nicholas came in with the first box. He dumped it on the table, and then shot her an amused look.

'You're not turning out to be a very conventional sort of nursemaid. Or a very sympathetic one,' he added.

'You don't need sympathy,' Cathryn retorted. 'In fact, it's probably not good for you. You've been a lot better since I've been around to shout at you and hassle you.'

Nicholas looked at her reflectively. 'You could be right about that,' he said at last. 'Although I don't think this was the sort of care and attention Charles had in mind when he asked you to look after me! He was expecting you to dole out a lot of solicitude and kind words.'

'I don't feel very kindly towards you at the moment!'

'You did last night,' he said softly.

That stopped her in her tracks. Cathryn's eyes became very wary and her mouth set into a dead-straight line as she looked at him.

'What exactly do you mean by that?'

'Precisely what I said,' Nicholas replied calmly. 'Last night, for just a few moments, you *did* feel kindly towards me. Very kindly.'

'I think that you must be confusing my reactions with your own,' Cathryn said in a very cool tone.

'I think our reactions were exactly the same. And

in case you're wondering—yes, that did surprise me as much as it surprised you.'

'I wasn't surprised about anything,' Cathryn denied, just a little too hastily. 'And I don't intend to be surprised in the future,' she warned him.

He didn't seem in the least perturbed by her response. 'We'll see,' was all he said. Then he turned towards the door. 'I'll fetch the rest of the boxes.'

Cathryn noticed that he was limping quite heavily, and her conscience gave a hefty twitch. 'I'll give you a hand,' she said in a subdued voice.

'You don't have to. I can manage.'

'I *want* to.' She glared at him fiercely. 'You are an exasperating man. Do you refuse all offers of help on principle?'

Nicholas shrugged. 'I suppose I'm just used to looking after myself. I've always done it, and I expect I always will.'

'That doesn't seem to leave much room for anyone else in your life.'

'No, it doesn't,' he agreed. 'Which is why I stick to short-term relationships. Remember that, Cathryn.'

She instantly bristled at the implication behind his words. 'I don't think that I'll *need* to remember it,' she said stiffly. Then, since the one advantage she had over him was mobility, she quickly walked on ahead, successfully putting an end to the conversation.

After they had brought the rest of the food up to the house and stacked it away, Nicholas announced that he was going to take a rest.

'You sleep an awful lot,' Cathryn observed with a frown. 'Is that all part of the delayed shock?'

'I think I'm over most of the shock by now. And I

don't really sleep much at all. Just an odd hour here and there. I never manage to sleep right through the night unless I take one of their damned pills.'

'Talking of pills,' said Cathryn, her frown deepening, 'you *are* taking all your medication, aren't you?'

Nicholas's eyebrows gently rose. 'I thought that was one the things you were meant to keep an eye on. Isn't it one of the main reasons Charles wanted you around? To make sure I don't skip any—or take too many?'

'I can't watch you every minute of the day. Anyway, you're an adult, not a child. You shouldn't *need* watching.'

'That isn't what my brother thinks.'

'I'm beginning to think that your brother doesn't know you very well,' she said frankly.

Nicholas looked thoughtful for a moment. 'Perhaps you ought to tell Charles that, the next time you see him,' he said at last.

'Why not tell him yourself?'

His expression became quite unreadable. 'That might be rather difficult. I might have been staying at my brother's flat, but Charles and I don't actually speak to each other unless we absolutely have to. We haven't done for five years.'

He limped out of the kitchen after that, putting a very definite end to the conversation. Cathryn sighed. If only she knew the cause of the rift between the two brothers, she might be able to stop saying the wrong thing every time the subject came up.

She pottered around the kitchen for a while, and then decided to go for a walk to get some fresh air. It was still bright outside, but cooler than it had been during the last few days. She pulled on the thick jacket she had brought with her, and then tramped off.

Now that Nicholas was back, she found she didn't mind being on the island so much. It had just been being here totally on her own that had so unnerved her. She climbed to the top of the hill that rose up behind Nicholas's house; then, puffing hard, she stood there and looked around.

From here she could see the third house, which was much larger than Nicholas's. She guessed that his friend, Hamish, must be fairly rolling in money. Owning a place like this, which didn't have any source of income except for the rent from a couple of houses, and a lot of daffodils which the absent Hamish didn't even bother to pick, had to be a very expensive hobby!

She could see that a place like this would appeal to a great many people, though. A small, self-contained kingdom—quite an ego-trip for whoever owned it! He really would be lord of all he surveyed.

But Cathryn hadn't yet succumbed to its charm. Perhaps the island would appeal to her more in the spring, when it would be covered in daffodils, and the trees and grass would be freshly green, instead of the rather jaded shades of late autumn.

She walked slowly back down the hill, and then made her way towards the beach. The island had a very rocky shoreline except for this small stretch on the landward side, where there were patches of sand and tiny rock pools. She wandered around for a while, picking up a couple of shells and stones with interesting markings. Then she grinned. She was acting like a child! She supposed no one ever really grew out of beachcombing, though.

It was hunger that finally drew her back to the house. She realised that she hadn't had a decent meal since she had left London. As she approached it, she saw that Nicholas was sitting outside, perched comfortably on the low wall that bound the patch of grass that passed for a front garden.

'Enjoy your walk?' he asked as she drew nearer.

Cathryn shrugged. 'It was all right, I suppose.'

'Getting to know the place?'

'There's not much to know, is there?' she retorted. 'I mean, basically it's a hummock stuck in the middle of the sea!'

If Nicholas was disappointed by her reply, he didn't show it. 'Some people take to it straight away, others take a lot longer,' he said comfortably.

'And I dare say some never take to it at all,' she said pointedly.

'We can't all like the same things,' he replied in an unruffled voice.

Cathryn studied his relaxed features. 'It certainly seems to agree with you,' she commented. 'You've been in a much better temper since we've been here. I keep expecting you to make some really nasty remark, and you don't.'

'Was I really that bad before?' Nicholas asked in what seemed like perfectly genuine surprise.

'You weren't exactly a fun person to have around!'

He seemed to consider her reply. 'Perhaps I'm more myself when I'm on this island,' he suggested at last.

'You mean that I'm seeing the real Nicholas Ellis?' she enquired with some scepticism.

'Something like that. I'm not usually a pill-popping invalid,' he added, with an unexpected grin.

Cathryn's brows drew together. 'You really *have* changed since we've been here. You've even started to make jokes!'

'Believe it or not, I'm reputed to have quite a sense of humour. It's just that I seem to have lost it these last few months.'

'Well, I suppose that driving over a land-mine has got to have *some* side-effects,' she said philosophically. She seated herself on the wall beside him, and then lifted her face to the sun. 'Mm, this is nice,' she murmured. 'I love Indian summers. They make the winter seem shorter.' She had briefly closed her eyes against the glare of the sun. When she opened them again, she found that Nicholas was looking at her in a way that she found vaguely disturbing. 'Er—how much longer are we going to stay on the island?' she asked, suddenly wanting to keep the conversation moving along safe lines.

'Another day. Maybe two, if the weather holds,' he said. His gaze became thoughtful. 'Why don't you like it here?'

'I don't know. Perhaps it's just too peaceful and quiet.'

'Are you really that much of a city girl? Were you born in London?'

'No,' Cathryn admitted. 'I was born in a small town about fifty miles away. I moved to London when I got my first job, and I've lived there ever since.'

'What about your family?' asked Nicholas. 'Or don't you have any? You've never mentioned them.'

'You've never asked before now,' replied Cathryn. 'I didn't think you were that interested! But, if you really want to know, I'm an only child and both my parents are still alive.'

'Do you see them often?'

'Not often. But I go back home when I can, and I keep in touch by phone.' She looked at him curiously. 'Why do you want to know?'

'People's backgrounds are often a clue as to what makes them tick.'

'Well, my background's very ordinary. I had a happy childhood, and nothing very dramatic ever happened to me. The only problem was that my parents had me quite late in life. Like a lot of older parents with an only child, they were very overprotective. That's fine when you're a kid and you're the centre of attention, but not so good as you get older. I knew that if I wanted to be independent, then I was going to have to get away. They didn't like it, or approve, when I told them I was moving out,' she admitted, her brows drawing together as she remembered what a difficult time it had been. 'But I think, in the end, they understood that I wasn't going because I didn't love them. And I really couldn't have stayed at home any longer. It sounds an awful thing to say, but they were suffocating me with love and kindness.'

'If they were that overprotective, you must have been fairly naïve and inexperienced when you first came to London.'

'Well, no one would have looked at me and marked me down as sophisticated,' she agreed drily.

'That kind of girl's easy bait for a certain type of man,' Nicholas comented.

Cathryn was suddenly wary, wondering where

this conversation was beginning to lead. 'I suppose so,' she agreed after a short pause.

'So—who was he?'

She decided it would be safer to pretend ignorance. 'What are you on about?'

'You're not naïve *now*, Cathryn,' he said firmly. 'You know perfectly well who I mean. The man who convinced you that you don't like sex.'

'I really don't know how we got on to this subject——' she began stiffly.

'We got on to it because I'm interested,' he interrupted her. 'And because I think you need to tell someone about it. My guess is that you've never told anyone. If your parents are as old-fashioned as you say, you certainly couldn't discuss it with them, and you don't seem to have any friends.'

'I've got friends,' Cathryn said hotly. 'Good friends!'

'But you've never talked to them about this, have you?' he challenged her.

'There was nothing to say!' She glared at him fiercely, but he stared right back at her and she was the first one to look away. 'At least, nothing very original,' she muttered. 'I was stupid and I was inexperienced, and I got hurt. It's something that happens every day. Hundreds—*thousands*—of people could tell the same boring tale. I thought I was in love, but he was only interested in the chase. When he'd got what he wanted—and he wasn't even very *good* at it—then it was goodbye, Cathryn, and on to the next one.'

'Poor Cathryn,' Nicholas said softly.

But she didn't want his sympathy. 'I got over it,' she insisted. 'And at least it taught me that men really are a different species. You don't catch women needing to mark notches on their bedposts just to boost their egos!'

'You're right about the male ego,' agreed Nicholas, to her amazement. 'It is a pretty frail thing.'

'You're willing to admit that?' she said disbelievingly. 'I never thought I'd hear a man say that!'

'Why not?' He gave the very faintest of grins. 'Just because we're male, that doesn't make us perfect. And a lot of women don't appreciate how much a man has to rely on his physical responses. A woman can always fake it. A man never can, and that makes us peculiarly vulnerable.'

'You're putting that forward as an excuse?' Cathryn said in some disgust.

'Not an excuse—just an explanation. If a man fails in bed, then it's embarrassingly obvious to both himself and whoever he's with. And I suppose that fear of failure is always there, even if it's tucked away at the very back of the mind.'

Cathryn's eyebrows shot up. 'Even yours?'

'Even mine,' he agreed equably. 'And to some men it's a very real and constant fear. They might not even be aware of it. They might seem outwardly brimming with confidence. It's still there, though, locked away in their subconscious. And when that happens, every woman they meet turns into a sort of challenge. They need to prove to themselves over and over that everything's fine and still functioning adequately.'

'I suppose I never thought of it that way,' Cathryn conceded grudgingly.

'It doesn't excuse their behaviour, of course,' Nicholas went on. 'But in a way, you can almost feel sorry for them, because they find it very hard to form any kind of meaningful relationship. As you said, it's always goodbye, Cathryn—or Sue, Lucy or Jenny— and on to the next. They think they're notching up sexual conquests, and can't see that it's actually a weakness.'

'It's still pretty rough on women, when they run into a man like that,' pointed out Cathryn.

'Yes, it is. But since it's virtually impossible to change human nature, women are just going to have to go on coping with it as best they can.' Nicholas's gaze rested on her thoughtfully. 'How did you cope, Cathryn?'

'I just sort of muddled through it. And in the end, I got over it.' She lifted her head a little defiantly. 'I'm a lot tougher than I look.'

He shook his head, though. 'No, I don't think you're tough. A little disillusioned, perhaps. And you've definitely got some scars that haven't quite faded yet. But whoever the bastard was, he knocked something out of you. Perhaps it's time we tried to put it back again,' he suggested softly.

Her ears instantly pricked up. 'We?' she repeated warily. 'How did this suddenly turn into a double-act?'

'It's not something that you can put right on your own,' Nicholas pointed out with a returning touch of humour.

'Nothing needs to be put right!' Cathryn insisted very firmly. 'I'm fine the way I am.'

'You're not doing too badly,' he agreed. 'But things could be a lot better.'

'How?' As soon as she'd said it, Cathryn knew that she shouldn't have asked.

'For a start, you could admit that you like to be kissed.'

'Kissed by whom?' she said scathingly. 'By you? It was OK, you know, but hardly earth-shattering.'

To her amazement, he didn't react to her rudeness. 'We could try again,' he suggested, his green eyes glinting. 'I'd like to be able to say I made the earth move for you!'

Despite herself, the corners of Cathryn's mouth curled into a smile.

'You've a nice mouth when you smile,' Nicholas murmured. 'In fact, it even looks nice when you're in a bad mood.'

He leant forward a little, and Cathryn immediately moved back. 'Remember what the doctors said,' she warned. 'No excitement!'

'Then how about a very unexciting kiss?'

But Cathryn wasn't sure that such a thing existed, as far as Nicholas Ellis was concerned. And she didn't think this was a good time to find out!

'It's getting chilly,' she said, jumping a little too briskly to her feet. 'I think it's time we went back to the house.'

Although it was the very last thing she had expected, Nicholas nodded in agreement and stood up. He followed her up the path and through the front door. At the end of the hall, though, he stopped her from going through to the kitchen by sliding an arm lazily around her waist.

'What are you doing?' she squeaked rather unnecessarily, because it was very obvious what he was doing.

Nicholas didn't even bother to answer. Instead, he took a slow, deliberate kiss from her, his lips moving over hers almost thoughtfully, as if gauging his own reaction as well as hers.

'Mmm,' he murmured at last. 'Not unexciting at all.'

Cathryn had to agree with him about that. Not that she intended to tell him to his face, of course! He seemed to have a fairly high opinion of himself, as it was. She didn't intend to add to it.

'I suppose it was all right,' she said stiffly.

'No more than "all right"?' he mocked lightly. 'Then how about this?'

And 'this' turned out to be a kiss of a very different calibre. More urgent, more demanding—more everything! Cathryn thought with a gulp. Then, for quite some time, she didn't seem capable of thinking anything at all.

When the kiss finally came to an end, she experienced an odd surge of relief mixed with disappointment. Then her nerves began to jangle out a warning all over again, because it wasn't over at all. Nicholas had simply moved on to other things.

With an expertise that shook her a little, he had her jacket undone, and the thickness of her jumper yielded easily to the hands that slid beneath it.

'Don't *do* that,' she said furiously.

But his hands didn't retreat an inch. 'Why not?' he asked huskily. 'You're very nice to touch.' His fingers eased upwards and tickled the underside of her breast. 'Touching can be fun,' he added persuasively. 'And at this stage, it's really very innocent.'

But Cathryn was suddenly afraid to concede anything at all to him. 'Remember the doctors' orders,' she reminded him again sharply.

'I'm still not overexcited,' he assured her, with a

gleam of pure wickedness. 'You'd know if I were,' he purred meaningfully.

And that was true, since he was standing extremely close now. His fingers lightly tickled again, and Cathryn closed her eyes a little desperately. This could so easily get out of hand, and there was no one around to stop it.

You can stop it, said a small voice inside her head. If you want to, it added maliciously.

I do, she breathed. I *do*. But it didn't sound very convincing, not even to herself. For some reason, this man seemed to be able to get to her. It was ridiculous, really, because in a lot of ways he was still a stranger. But he didn't feel like a stranger when he touched her, and perhaps that was the most unsettling thing of all.

Nicholas seemed to tire of waiting for her to sort out her confused thoughts. To amuse himself, he began a series of light, nibbling kisses around the nape of her neck, pushing back the collar of her jacket so he could more easily reach her warm, soft skin.

Unfamiliar tingles curled their way down Cathryn's spine, and she was finding it just a little difficult to breathe.

You didn't come here for this, she told herself, a trifle frantically. You're meant to be looking after this man! He's an invalid, not long out of hospital. . .

But he certainly wasn't behaving like an invalid! And if he continued like this for much longer she had the feeling that he was going to forget all about the instructions that the doctors had given him.

She managed to push herself away from him. 'I think we ought to stop this right now, and instead have something to eat,' she said in a distinctly shaky voice. 'We haven't had a proper meal since we've been here. Are you hungry?'

'Definitely,' he confirmed, his eyes glinting very brightly. There were lines of amusement around his mouth, but something in his voice warned her that part of him was taking this very seriously indeed.

'I'll go and see what's in the cupboard,' she muttered, anxious to escape.

'I think that you ought to stay exactly where you are for a few more minutes.'

'Why?'

'So I can do this,' Nicholas answered smoothly. He moved in on her again with unexpected swiftness, taking his weight on his good leg so that he could more easily keep his balance. In fact, it was Cathryn who ended up completely off balance—and in more ways than one! His assault on her this time was all the more deadly because he was no longer teasing her. No more light kisses or playful tickling. His kisses were fierce enough to take away her breath, and his hands shifted over her with open enjoyment, savouring the warm softness they found, touching and taking with hungry delight.

'Still not interested in sex, Cathryn?' Nicholas murmured in her ear.

Instantly, she stiffened. His words had reminded her all too vividly that men did this sort of thing just for a game. And she wasn't playing a second time!

Nicholas sensed her tension at once, and raised his head. 'Wrong thing to say?' he said ruefully.

'No, it was exactly the *right* thing,' Cathryn replied coldly. 'For a few moments there, I almost forgot that you're no different from all the rest.'

Nicholas looked at her steadily. 'No different at all?' he challenged her softly.

But all of Cathryn's defences were back in place again now. She forced the persuasiveness of his kisses out of her mind, and answered him in a very clear voice. 'The only difference I can see is that the last man I knew wasn't very good at this, while you are. But then, you've probably had a lot more practice.'

For just a moment, his green eyes gleamed brightly in warning. Then the light died away again, and he drew back from her.

'I suppose I asked for that,' he said in a cool voice. 'And you're right, I'm not offering any more than all the rest.' He paused, then went on, 'I suppose I ought to apologise.'

She certainly hadn't expected that. 'Apologise?' she said, her eyebrows shooting up.

'I shouldn't have started this. I don't know why I did.' He began to look rather restless now, moving back another couple of paces and frowning slightly. 'I certainly never intended anything like this when I asked you to drive me down here.'

'Didn't you?' Her mouth curled in clear scepticism. 'Perhaps you had it in mind all along. In fact, ever since you accused me of being interested in your brother!'

At that, Nicholas's gaze swung round to fix on her unswervingly. 'What the hell do you mean by that?' he demanded.

Cathryn stared straight back at him. 'It's a well-known fact that there's always a lot of rivalry between brothers. Perhaps you don't want Charles to have anything that you haven't had!'

She had expected Nicholas to be angry at her accusation. What she hadn't expected was the flare of pure rage that crossed his face. An instant later, he gripped her arm so hard that she almost yelped out loud. 'I always thought you knew more than you let on,' he said in a totally grim tone. 'Who told you? Not Charles!' he stated with utter certainty. 'He'd never speak about it to anyone. So, who else knows about it? Who *could* know?' he muttered with a black frown. Then he gave her a hard shake. 'Tell me, Cathryn!'

But she didn't have the slightest idea what he was talking about. All she did know was that he was suddenly in an absolutely towering rage, and that Nicholas Ellis in this mood frightened her half to death.

'N-no one's told me anything,' she stuttered. 'I don't know what you're on about. Or why I said that. I suppose I was just angry at you because I thought you were using me. Taking what you wanted, without giving a damn about how *I* felt about it, and what *I* wanted.'

Very slowly, Nicholas let go of her. 'Is that the truth?' he demanded.

'Yes!' And it certainly was. Cathryn wouldn't have dared to lie to him, not while he looked like that. She was still shaking a little, but getting a small amount of courage back again now. 'Why did you react like that?' she asked unsteadily. 'What did I say to make you so furious?'

'You accused me of wanting whatever Charles has,' he reminded her, his own tone still edged with anger. 'I thought that, somehow, someone had found out. That it had become a matter for common gossip.'

'I don't understand this,' frowned Cathryn. '*What* could I have found out?'

Nicholas green gaze fixed on her. 'The reason why my brother hasn't wanted to speak to me for the last five years. You see, Charles thought exactly the same as you. That I wanted what he had.'

'What did he have that you could possibly have wanted?' asked Cathryn in a puzzled voice.

'Helena,' replied Nicholas tightly. 'The beautiful, dead Helena. Charles believes that I once had an affair with his wife.'

CHAPTER SEVEN

CATHRYN was beginning to wish very fervently that she had never got involved with these two brothers. The relationship between them was too complicated, too full of pitfalls into which an outsider could so easily step.

'Why would your brother think something like that?' she asked jerkily.

Nicholas held her gaze levelly. 'Because all the evidence seemed to point to it.'

'And *did* you have an affair?' Cathryn had blurted out the question before she could stop herself, but she dearly wished it had remained unspoken.

He didn't answer straight away. Instead, he studied her face for a few moments, as if searching for something. 'What do you think?' he said at last.

This time, it was Cathryn who took a long time answering. She thought very hard about it first, and forced herself to be objective. 'I don't think you'd do anything like that,' she said at length. 'I don't think you'd *need* to.

Nicholas visibly relaxed a fraction. 'Why not?' he asked.

'Because you don't seem like the type of man who has to prove anything. Not to yourself, or to anyone else.'

And this time, amazingly, a faint smile showed on Nicholas's face. 'That sounds almost like a compliment.'

'I suppose it is,' Cathryn conceded. Then she gave a light frown. 'Are you going to tell me how your brother got such a wrong idea about you?'

To her disappointment, he shook his head. 'I think I've had enough soul-searching for one day. Let the family skeletons stay in their closet for a while longer.' He glanced at his watch. 'You said you were going to get something to eat. I think that's a good idea. We've already missed lunch—in fact, it's almost dinnertime.'

She shot an incredulous look at him. 'After all this, how can you think about your stomach?'

'Quite easily,' Nicholas replied, with an unexpected grin. 'I seem to be recovering all of my appetites since we've been here!'

Cathryn realised that she wasn't going to get any more information out of him. In fact, she was astonished that he had told her as much as he had. This island certainly seemed to do something to people! Nicholas had unwound to an amazing degree since their arrival.

And have you unwound as well? murmured a voice inside her head.

She swallowed hard. She supposed she had. Kissing Nicholas—and *enjoying* it. And who knew where it might have led, if it hadn't suddenly turned sour?

As she walked slowly towards the kitchen, she was more unsettled by that last thought than by Nicholas's explanation of the deep rift between himself and his brother. Nothing about this trip was turning out the way she had expected. More and more, she was getting a strong feeling that she ought to back away from all this, before it was too late.

Too late for what? she found herself wondering

uneasily. She didn't know—and that was the main problem. Things were happening; the situation was somehow changing. She didn't know exactly where she was heading any longer, and that disturbed her deeply.

As they reached the kitchen, she suddenly swung round to confront Nicholas. 'I'd like to go back to London,' she said bluntly. 'I don't want to stay here any longer.'

'Because of me?'

His question hung softly in the air between them. Cathryn had the feeling that, whichever way she answered it, she was going to be giving something away. In the end, she said nothing, but she suspected that had told him something as well.

'It's too late to leave today,' Nicholas said at last, when it became obvious that she wasn't going to answer him. 'But, if you like, we can leave first thing in the morning.'

'Just like that?' she said in surprise. 'No arguments? You're not going to try and persuade me to change my mind? Or stay on here by yourself?'

He gave a brief shrug. 'Perhaps coming down here wasn't such a good idea,' he answered rather enigmatically. Then he glanced out of the window. 'Anyway, I think the weather's going to change.'

'The sky's still blue and the sun's shining,' Cathryn pointed out.

'There's a different feel to the air. I think the Indian summer's over.'

Cathryn was certain he was wrong; the weather looked absolutely fine to her. She wasn't going to argue with him, though. He had agreed to leave, and that was the important thing, as far as she was concerned.

By the time they sat down to eat their meal, there was a dark smudge of cloud right across the sky, and a light breeze was stirring the trees behind the house. Cathryn hoped the sea wouldn't be too rough by the morning. It wasn't far to the mainland, but there would still be plenty of time for her to get seasick!

Nicholas took himself off to his room after dinner. She didn't know if he planned to sleep, or if he was going to work on the manuscript of his book, which he had brought with him. She didn't really care too much which it was. She was just glad to be free of his company for a while. She hadn't even enjoyed her dinner very much, sitting across the table from him and seeing that green gaze every time she looked up. There was something about him which was disturbing her more and more. He only had to come near her and her skin twitched in a really odd way!

There was a portable television in the lounge, and she watched that for much of the evening. She wasn't particularly interested in the programmes, but at least they helped to keep her mind off other things.

She was just thinking about going up to bed when Nicholas strolled in. He must be a mind-reader, she thought to herself a little shakily.

He took very little notice of her, though. Instead, he went over to the window and looked out.

Cathryn had glanced out of the window earlier, and she could have told him that there was very little to see. The light breeze had turned into a wind, which was sending clouds scudding across the sky. They were thick enough to obscure the moon for much of the time, so it was pretty dark out there.

'Did you see the weather forecast?' Nicholas asked rather abruptly.

Cathryn shrugged. 'I think it was on. To be honest, though, I didn't listen to it.' She didn't want to admit that her thoughts had been somewhere else entirely.

At that, he rounded on her, a deep frown darkening his face. 'In a place like this, you *always* pay attention to the weather.' Then his flash of temper vanished as quickly as it had appeared. 'Not that it really matters too much,' he muttered. 'We can't get off here until the morning.'

He sounded as if he would be very pleased if someone waved a magic wand and whisked him off right now. Cathryn nibbled her lower lip. Was it because of her? She really didn't see how it could be. Those kisses he had given her earlier might have made him feel restless, but she was sure he was more than capable of coping with physical frustration. *She* was the one who, to her utter amazement, seemed to be having problems with it.

Perhaps it was because she had never truly encountered it before. Nicholas's kisses had done something to her. Innocent though they had seemed at the time, they had started a small, gnawing ache inside of her. She had hardly noticed it at first. Now she could hardly think of anything else.

She wished he would leave the room. It would be easier to think straight if he weren't around. A couple of minutes later, he did just that, and in only seconds she found herself wishing he would come back again.

Cathryn got rather abruptly to her feet. This was perfectly ridiculous! She would go upstairs, have a bath, and then get a good night's sleep. She was tired, that was all. Everyone had fanciful thoughts when they were tired. It was a well-known fact.

The bath water was cool, and the sheets even icier than the night before. Cathryn's teeth actually chattered as she tried to get warm. And the wind had taken on a more strident note now. She could hear it whipping through the trees and throwing itself against her window, making the frames rattle.

Oh, this was really great, she thought irritably. If it went on all night, she wasn't going to get a single wink of sleep! Resolutely, she closed her eyes and tried to ignore the cold, the weather, and the confused thoughts whirling round inside her head. And in the end she was successful, sliding into a rather restless sleep.

She was woken up some time later by the sound of something hammering against the window. For a few moments, she lay there in the darkness, blinking blearily and wondering what on earth it was. Then she realised it was rain. It was pouring! And the wind had risen to a steady howl as it pounded its way across the island and whipped around the house.

Outside, several small objects seemed to be crashing about. Cathryn listened to the noises nervously, wondering how long this sudden storm was going to last. Then there was a much louder crash than all the rest. With a squeak of alarm, she scrambled out of bed and hurried over to switch on the light. She would feel a lot better if she could see what was going on!

When she clicked down the light switch, though, nothing happened. Another crash from outside set her heart thumping even faster. She fumbled with the door, finally found the handle, and flung it open.

Like the bedroom, the tiny landing was in pitch darkness. She couldn't see a thing; she could only hear the sounds of the storm steadily building in intensity.

A little frantically, she groped for the stairs. Perhaps the lights would come on downstairs. Even if they didn't, she might be able to find some matches, candles, *anything* that would give off some light and help to get rid of this awful suffocating darkness.

She let out an enormous sigh of relief as she finally found the top step of the stairs. She tried to go down too quickly, though, and tripped. With a loud howl of fear, she hurtled down half a dozen steps. She flung out one of her arms and just managed to grab hold of the banister, which stopped her from bumping and rolling her way right to the bottom.

Shaken and bruised, Cathryn huddled there in the darkness and felt like bawling her head off. She hated this storm, she hated this island, and she wished she were a million miles from here!

A door crashed open above her and a moment later Nicholas's voice boomed out in the darkness. 'What the hell's going on? Cathryn? Where are you?'

'Halfway down the stairs!' she managed to get out in a ragged voice.

'What on earth are you doing there?'

'Breaking my neck, I think,' she replied dolefully.

A few moments later he was beside her. Cathryn at last began to relax. Nicholas was here—perhaps things would begin to improve from now on. Then she jumped violently as she felt his hands run over her.

'What are you *doing*?' she demanded in a shrill voice.

'Checking that you haven't broken any bones,' he answered.

Cathryn wriggled away from him. 'I haven't!' she said with great certainty. She glared at him in the darkness, hardly able to see the pale smudge of his face. 'Are you sure this isn't just an excuse to grope me?'

'No, I'm not certain of that at all,' replied Nicholas cheerfully. 'Can you get up?'

With a faint groan, Cathryn managed it. She might not have broken anything, but she was certainly going to have some hefty bruises.

'Why are you wandering around in the dark?' Nicholas asked her.

'I didn't like the storm,' she said defensively. 'And it was so noisy! It sounded as if the roof were crashing in. And when I tried to turn on the light, nothing happened.'

'In other words, you were just plain scared,' Nicholas said in an unexpectedly gentle voice.

'Yes, I was,' she admitted rather crossly.

'Well, we can't stay here all night, in the middle of the stairs. Shall we go up or down?'

'Down,' Cathryn decided rather hastily. Upstairs there were only the bedrooms, and she didn't think it would be a very good idea to spend much time there with Nicholas—especially in this darkness!

She hobbled her way carefully down the rest of the stairs, wincing a little as her bruised bones began to ache. 'Why won't the lights come on?' she asked, as she felt her way into the lounge.

'Something must have knocked out the generator,' replied Nicholas. 'Wait here, I'll get some candles.'

He was only gone for a couple of minutes, but it seemed like very much longer to Cathryn. She stood there listening to the force of the storm hurling itself against the house, and shivered. Some people might like all this nature-in-the-raw, but she definitely didn't. And when she saw Nicholas returning with a flickering light, her knees positively sagged with relief. It was so marvellous to be able to see again, even if the candle did only throw out a very feeble glow.

Nicholas lit a couple more candles, placing them around the room. Then he came to sit on the sofa beside her.

'Better?' he asked.

'I suppose so.' Cathryn shivered again. 'I can't wait to get out of here.'

'It's only a storm.'

'But it sounds so—oh, I don't know. So *violent*.'

Nicholas looked at her. 'You don't like violence?'

'Of course not. Does anyone?'

'I suppose not,' he said slowly. 'Although it is possible to—get used to it.'

Something in his tone of voice made her look at him sharply. 'Have *you* got used to it?'

He shrugged. 'In a way—yes. In my job, I've seen so much of it.'

Cathryn wrinkled her nose. 'I don't know how you can keep on doing a job like yours, always seeing the worst side of human nature, the civil wars, the riots, people trying to maim and kill each other.' She gave a small shudder. 'There must be days when the whole world seems like an evil place.'

'It does get to you at times,' Nicholas admitted. 'And I've seen correspondents and journalists who just can't take any more, and have to give it up.'

'You haven't reached that point, though?'

'No. It might happen at some time in the future, but right now I still enjoy my job, and I intend to carry on with it.'

'Even though you nearly got blown to bits because of it?' she said a little incredulously.

'There's a risk in just about everything we do,' replied Nicholas. 'People have accidents in cars, in the home, when they're away on holiday—the list is endless. Short of staying in bed all day, there's no way to make sure you're completely safe.' His eyes gleamed. 'And even a bed can be a risky place if you're sharing it with the wrong person.'

'Someone like Mandy?' Cathryn remarked a little caustically, remembering the slinky blonde who had gatecrashed Sir Charles's flat.

'She'd certainly be a danger to anyone with high blood-pressure,' agreed Nicholas, the corners of his mouth curling upwards. Then his brows drew together again. 'Do you dislike the kind of work I do?' he asked in a very different tone. 'Or disapprove of it?'

'Of course not. People have to know what's going on in the world, even if a lot of it isn't very nice. It's no good ignoring it, pretending it doesn't exist. I just wish. . .'

'Wish what?' he asked, as her voice trailed away.

'Well—I wish it wasn't *you* who had to do it,' she blurted out. 'Investigative reporting is all very well, but you're not going to do much good if you get yourself killed!'

'I'll be more careful next time, I promise,' he said with a dry smile. 'And my job isn't all doom and gloom. I've seen some extraordinary acts of heroism, and met a lot of people who are actually trying to make the world a better place.'

'I wish someone would make *this* part of the world a better place,' she said with a grimace, as another gust of wind shook the house. 'Is it my imagination, or is the storm getting stronger?'

'The worst will probably be over in an hour or so. And we're quite safe inside this house. It's already weathered the storms of over a century. One more won't blow it down.'

'Are you sure of that?' muttered Cathryn nervously, as another wild howl of wind rattled the doors and windows. 'I'm really looking forward to getting back to the mainland!'

'There may be one or two problems there,' Nicholas warned.

'Problems?' she repeated edgily. 'What sort of problems?'

'A wind like this always whips up very heavy seas. I doubt if we'll be able to make the crossing tomorrow.'

'You mean we'll be stuck here another day?' she said in alarm.

Nicholas didn't seem particularly concerned by the prospect. 'We've plenty of food, and wood for the fire. We can easily get by for another day or two.'

'I thought it was going to be just one more day! Now you're talking about two. Which is it?' she demanded.

'I don't know,' he said with complete honesty. 'I don't have any control over the weather.'

'No, you don't,' she agreed tightly. 'But it *is* your fault that we're going to be stranded here. You should have realised this storm was coming, and got us off in time. In fact, you shouldn't even have brought us here in the first place. This is a ridiculous time of year to go flitting off to an island. Everyone knows you get storms in the autumn!'

Nicholas studied her thoughtfully. 'What's brought on this little outburst? The thought of being stuck here for another day or so? Or is it because you'll be stranded here with *me*?' he finished softly.

Cathryn's hands fluttered ineffectually. She didn't know how to answer his question without telling him more than she wanted him to know. While she was still trying to think of the right words, another loud crash from outside made her jump, and by the time her jangled nerves had settled down again she found Nicholas was holding her shaking hands within his own.

'I can't do anything about the storm,' he murmured. 'But I might be able to make you forget it for a while.'

Cathryn had the feeling that his quiet offer was the most dangerous she had ever had. And it was frightening how tempted she was to accept it.

'No, thank you,' she forced herself to say in a polite voice.

'Any particular reason for your refusal?'

'I don't have to give reasons!' she said indignantly. 'Even though I've got several very good ones.'

'Such as the fact that you're still annoyed that I once accused you of chasing after my brother?' Nicholas suggested calmly.

'That certainly didn't make me like you any better!'

'What if I told you that I don't think that any more?
That I'm willing to accept that you work for my
brother, and that's all?'

Cathryn stared at him suspiciously. 'What made
you change your mind about me?'

'I don't really know,' he said with an odd smile.
'Except perhaps that you're just not cold and calcu-
lating enough to be a fortune-hunter.'

'I might be very good at acting,' she pointed out
stiffly.

Nicholas immediately shook his head. 'No, you're
not good at it at all. It's usually fairly easy to guess
what you're thinking and feeling.'

And that was a highly disturbing thing to hear him
say. To cover her confusion, Cathryn sat up very
straight and tried to withdraw her hands from his.

'The storm seems to be dying down a bit. I—I
think I'll go back to bed now and try to get some
sleep.'

Nicholas held on to her chilly fingers very firmly.
'The storm hasn't even hit its peak yet. I think you'd
feel a lot better if you stayed down here with me.'

'I'm tired,' she insisted.

He tossed a couple of cushions towards the end of
the sofa, to act as pillows.

'Then lie down here,' he invited.

'It's—it's too cold,' Cathryn said quickly.

'I'll get a couple of blankets, and light the fire.'

He was as good as his word. Minutes later, logs
were crackling in the grate and he had fished a
couple of blankets out of a cupboard. Cathryn
wrapped one around her shoulders. She had rushed
out of the bedroom in just her nightshirt, and was
genuinely freezing now.

'This house is like a fridge,' she grumbled. 'I haven't been warm since I got here. And I've been absolutely frozen at night.'

'You really need something to keep you warm,' Nicholas agreed.

'What do you suggest?' she asked scathingly. 'A hot-water bottle? Unfortunately, I didn't bring one with me. I didn't know you were bringing me to a place that hasn't got any proper heating!'

'A hot-water bottle's fine, if there's one around. Failing that, the best thing is to curl up with someone else.'

But Cathryn wasn't falling for that one. 'I'm fine with this blanket,' she said firmly.

'But I'm not,' Nicholas pointed out. 'Under this bathrobe, I'm wearing nothing at all. I'm getting cold.'

'Then move nearer to the fire.'

'I'd rather move nearer to you.'

'There isn't room!'

'There's plenty of room,' he contradicted her comfortably. Before she could get out another protest, he slid down on to the sofa beside her.

With the back of the sofa behind her and Nicholas sprawled out on her other side, Cathryn found herself trapped.

'Don't panic,' he advised her lazily. 'You're not in any danger, you know. If things get too hot, you can always make a bolt for it. You can run a lot faster than I can,' he reminded her.

Somehow, that didn't make Cathryn feel any safer. What if she didn't *want* to run?

Fresh rain slammed against the windows and the wind was positively screeching its way across the island. Yet the room they were in seemed surprisingly cosy, with the candles providing soft light and the fire crackling warmly. Cathryn should have been feeling very relaxed by now, but she certainly wasn't. And the man comfortably stretched out beside her was entirely responsible for her unsettled frame of mind.

Nicholas leant over and very gently kissed her mouth. The candlelight reflected on his face, and Cathryn suddenly realised how familiar his features seemed to her. And how very much she liked the warm touch of his lips. For some reason, that made her even more tense, and Nicholas felt the stiffening of her muscles.

'There's nothing to worry about,' he murmured. 'I'm still obeying doctors' orders, and being careful not to get overexcited.'

'I'm glad to hear it,' Cathryn said edgily.

'On the other hand,' he went on thoughtfully, 'there are quite a lot of things we can do that are very pleasant without being *too* stimulating.'

'I don't think I want to know about them!'

'Don't you?' Nicholas didn't sound in the least convinced. 'I get the impression that you're growing very curious, Cathryn.'

'Curious about what?' she couldn't help asking.

'About yourself. And the way you're reacting to me.'

'Nonsense!' she retorted crisply. 'Why on earth should I be curious about a thing like that?'

'Because that bad experience you had convinced you that you just weren't interested in sex. Now, you're beginning to wonder if you were wrong about that. If sex with the right person could be OK. Or even better than OK.'

'And you think you're that right person?' she said, somehow managing to make her tone sound scathing.

'No, I'm not the right person at all,' Nicholas replied, to her total astonishment. 'Our lifestyles don't fit together in any way. We like different things, *want* different things. But on a purely physical plane we're compatible, and I think that's starting to interest you.'

His rather cold-blooded analysis both fascinated and disturbed her. How devastating it would be to fall in love with a man like this, she thought to herself with a small inner shiver. Someone who could make love with his mind and his body, but not with his heart.

She half turned away from him, but he put out one arm and stopped her. At the same time, his fingers smoothly undid the top button of her nightshirt and slid inside.

'Just lie still,' he instructed as he felt her quiver. 'I'm not going to do anything very much. Just convince you that you don't have an real hang-ups.'

'I don't think I need convincing of that,' she managed to get out through teeth that had started to chatter slightly.

'Yes, you do,' he replied calmly. 'I don't want to see you go through the rest of your life thinking that you can't enjoy physical closeness with a man.'

The front of her nightshirt flapped open and Nicholas leant over her. Cathryn went to pull the material together again, but her hands didn't quite make it in time. Nicholas's mouth reached her first, and he proceeded to leave a trail of very light kisses from the base of her throat right down to the swell of her breast, where he lingered for a moment before leaving one final soft kiss on the taut dark pink nipple.

His kisses might have been light, but they still seemed to leave tiny scorch marks on her skin. When he looked as if he was going to move closer again, Cathryn suddenly panicked and tried to push him away. Nicholas didn't say a word. Instead, he caught hold of her hands and held them gently inside his own; then he rhythmically rubbed her palms, pressed his warm fingertips against her own, and finally stroked the back of her hands very lightly.

It was extraordinarily soothing. When he at last released her hands, Cathryn almost murmured in protest. He hadn't finished with her, though. His fingers moved lightly down to her ankles, circling and caressing the small, delicate bones. Then he gently tickled the soles of her feet, which sent an acute sensation of pleasure curling through her nerve-ends.

'Tiny hands and feet,' he commented softly. 'It's almost like making love to a doll.'

'Is that what you're doing?' she whispered in a dazed voice. 'Making love to me?'

'No, I'm not.'

At that, her eyes flew open. 'You're *not*?'

His mouth curled into one of his rare genuine smiles. 'I suppose I ought to be pretty pleased by the disappointment in your voice.'

'I'm not disappointed,' she denied hurriedly. 'I'm just——' She stopped right there, deciding that she didn't want to go into this any further. 'Well, what *are* you doing, then?'

'I think I'm getting very frustrated,' he said drily. 'But it's not an altogether unpleasant feeling.'

'If you moved away from me, things would no doubt improve,' she pointed out.

'Somehow, I don't think so. Anyway, I can live with it. I've managed for three months. I can go a little while longer.' He slid down beside her again. 'Turn on to your right side,' he instructed.

'Why?' she asked warily.

Nicholas sighed. 'Don't you ever do anything without an argument?'

Against her better judgement, Cathryn did as he had ordered. She heard him give a grunt of satisfaction, and then he curled up comfortably against her back.

'This way, we'll both keep warm,' he murmured. 'And one of us might get some sleep.'

Cathryn didn't know which one of them he meant, and she certainly had no intention of asking! She had to admit that it felt good, though, his relaxed body radiating warmth and an unexpected sense of security.

The storm howled on through the night, but it didn't disturb her. After just a few minutes, she was no longer awake to hear it.

CHAPTER EIGHT

WHEN Cathryn woke up in the morning, it took her a few moments to figure out where she was. And when she *did* finally figure it out, she gave a small gulp and sat up very quickly.

The first thing she discovered was that Nicholas was no longer lying on the sofa beside her. She was highly relieved at that. This man was getting rather hard to handle!

She pulled the blanket around her shoulders and padded over to the window. One glance outside confirmed her worst fears. The brunt of the storm was over, but the wind was still moaning softly over the island and the sea was heaving in a way that made her stomach lurch just to look at it.

'Great!' she muttered. 'We could be stuck here all winter!'

The fire had gone out, and the house was very cold again. With the generator on the blink, it meant there would be no hot water, no hot food—she couldn't even make herself a cup of coffee. Cathryn stared gloomily out of the window and fervently wished she were in a five-star hotel.

Just then, she saw Nicholas coming up the path. Her heart gave an odd little lurch and then settled down to a rhythm that was appreciably faster than usual, and she discovered that she felt sort of fluttery inside, which rather annoyed her. There was no need to get twitchy just because they had slept on the same sofa! After all, nothing had happened—*almost* nothing had happened, she corrected herself edgily. All the same, she wished she didn't have to face Nicholas in just a nightshirt and with a blanket wrapped round her. It made her feel at a distinct disadvantage. She would have felt more like the old composed and controlled Cathryn if she had been fully dressed.

Nicholas came through the front door, tossed his stick to one side, and then sat down in a nearby chair. Exercise still tired him, but he was moving about a lot easier now. He still used the stick most of the time, but Cathryn guessed he would be able to do without it fairly soon—she also guessed he was itching for that day to arrive. He wasn't the sort of man who would want to use props of any kind.

'Sleep well?' he enquired with a wolfish grin.

'Yes, thank you,' she said politely. 'And you?'

'Like a log,' he admitted. 'Although it was about the last thing I'd expected.'

'I suppose you took a couple of your sleeping pills?'

'That would be rather difficult,' replied Nicholas. 'I left them in London.'

Cathryn's eyebrows shot up. 'You forgot them?'

'No, I didn't forget them. I decided not to bring them with me.'

'But—you might have needed them!'

'I'm sick of taking pills,' Nicholas said calmly. 'So I've dumped them.'

She stared at him in alarm. '*All* of them?' she squeaked.

'Every last one,' he agreed cheerfully.

'But—what would your doctors say?'

'The doctors did a great job in patching me up. I don't need them to help put my head together, though,' Nicholas said firmly. 'I can do that for myself.'

'You were taking the pills in London,' she reminded him.

'Yes, I was. Pills to make me sleep, pills to keep me calm, pills to stop me thinking and feeling. But I *need* to think and feel. And I can handle it, even if some of the memories aren't too good. Haven't I been better company these last couple of days?' he challenged her.

Cathryn had to admit that there had certainly been a change in him. 'Well, I suppose you know what you're doing,' she said with a resigned shrug.

'I do,' Nicholas said with complete conviction. 'And now we've dealt with that, let's get down to more practical matters. The storm last night did quite a lot of damage. We're going to have to rough it for the next day or two.'

Cathryn wrinkled her nose. 'You can't fix the generator?'

'I can't even *get* to the generator,' he replied drily. 'It's housed in an old outbuilding round the back, and the whole thing's collapsed. Roof, walls—they're just a pile of rubble, and the generator's underneath it.'

'So, we'll be washing in cold water and eating cold food,' she said philosophically. 'Have you got any more bad news?'

Nicholas looked at her in surprise. 'You're taking this a lot better than I thought you would.'

'What did you expect,' she asked wryly. 'Hysterics? Temper? Neither of those will do a lot of good.'

'No, they won't,' he agreed. 'I didn't expect you to see it in quite that light, though.'

'Why not? Didn't your brother tell you that I've got a reputation for being calm and capable?'

'I seem to remember one or two occasions when you haven't been either of those things,' Nicholas murmured, his words bringing a warm flush to her face. 'But I'd better not get side-tracked—much as I'd like to be,' he added, with a gleam in his eyes. 'Anyway, there's something else that I haven't yet told you.'

'Not good news?' she guessed, looking at his face.

'Not good news,' Nicholas agreed. 'The boat's gone.'

'Gone?' she yelped. 'Gone where?'

'I've no idea. It must have broken away from its moorings during the height of the storm. By now, it'll either have sunk or have been smashed to matchwood.'

Cathryn swallowed hard. 'What—what are we going to do?' Her voice began to sound a little panicky. 'We're marooned!'

'It won't be for long. As soon as the weather begins to calm down, we'll send a signal to the mainland. Someone will see it, and come and get us.'

'What kind of signal?'

'Have you seen the flagpole behind the house?' She had, and remembered wondering what it was for. 'We run up a red flag if there's an emergency, and a yellow flag if we're in need of assistance,' Nicholas went on.

'Then I think you ought to go and run up a red flag right now!' Cathryn said nervously.

'Why? This isn't an emergency situation. I'll wait

until the sea's calmed down enough for them to put out a boat, and then run up the yellow flag to let them know we need some help.'

Cathryn supposed she would have to be satisfied with that. Yet she couldn't stop feeling edgy. She was stranded on this island with Nicholas—she couldn't even get away if she wanted to. For some reason, that made her *very* jumpy.

Rather to her surprise, though, the rest of the day passed without any problems. Nicholas rigged a tripod over the fire so they could warm up some food, and the burning logs gave an illusion of warmth and brightness, even though they only threw out a fairly small circle of heat.

During the evening, the wind at last began to ease off. Cathryn was very relieved, since its mournful howling had begun to get on her nerves. She went over to the window, but it was too dark to see if the heaving waves had begun to subside into a gentler swell.

'Do you suppose we'll be able to get off of here tomorrow?' she asked hopefully.

Nicholas came over and stood behind her. 'You're very anxious to get away from this island,' he commented. 'Or are you just anxious to get away from *me*?' he enquired more softly. When Cathryn didn't answer, he edged a little closer. 'It's still cold,' he pointed out smoothly. 'Do you think we ought to sleep on the sofa again tonight?'

'I'll be fine in my own room,' she replied at once, very firmly. 'All I'll need are a couple of extra blankets.'

'Sure?'

Was that regret in his voice? Cathryn couldn't be

certain. But she *wasn't* going to let him talk her into something that she would be bound to regret later.

'Absolutely sure,' she said, and hoped she had managed to put enough conviction into her tone.

'Would you like to know something rather odd?' remarked Nicholas. 'Last night, I slept better than I have for months. No nightmares, no waking up in a cold sweat—and all without the help of pills. Why do you suppose that was?'

'I've no idea,' Cathryn said a little warily.

'Nor have I.' And he did sound genuinely puzzled.

To her relief, he then moved away from her, as if he needed some time to himself to think it over. Taking advantage of his suddenly introspective mood, Cathryn grabbed a candle and scuttled towards the kitchen.

'I'll go and see if I can find something for supper,' she called back over her shoulder.

To her annoyance, Nicholas gave a low chuckle, as if he knew perfectly well that she was running away from him. She spent ages in the kitchen, and her feet dragged with reluctance when she finally made her way back to the lounge. As she walked through the doorway, she decided she didn't like the soft, flickering glow of the candles. There was something altogether too intimate about candlelight!

After they had eaten supper and she finally announced she was going up to bed, though, Nicholas let her go with no more than a brief 'Goodnight'. Cathryn was so astonished that she hovered in the doorway for a few moments, not quite able to believe he was going to let her go without any hassle. He didn't say another word, though, and so she finally heaved a deep sigh of relief and scurried up the stairs.

She washed in cold water by the light of a candle, and then gritted her teeth as she got into the freezing bed. For just an instant she found herself wistfully remembering how warm and cosy it had been, curled up on that sofa with Nicholas. Then she sternly pushed the memory right out of her head.

For quite some time she lay there in the darkness, listening rather tensely. She still half expected to hear a soft tap on her door, and was shocked to find she was almost disappointed when it didn't happen.

She turned on to her side and resolutely closed her eyes. Of course you're not disappointed! she lectured herself sternly. Stop thinking about Nicholas Ellis and get to sleep.

Eventually she managed to doze off, and didn't wake up again until daylight. A quick glance out of the window revealed that the wind had died down completely and the sea looked almost flat. It was raining, though. In fact, not just raining, but bucketing down.

Under the canopy of dark cloud, the island looked distinctly gloomy. That rather suited Cathryn's mood, which this morning was as bleak as the weather. She didn't know why, either. She was just aware that she felt out of sorts, as if something in her life wasn't quite right.

That's hardly surprising, she muttered to herself. *Nothing's* really been right since you met Nicholas.

She decided to put him out of her mind for as long as possible. Not that that would be too long, she thought with a fresh wave of depression. She was bound to bump into him as soon as she went downstairs.

She began to turn away from the window, but at the last moment a flicker of movement caught her attention. She peered more closely through the rain-streaked glass, and realised that someone was moving around on the hillside behind the house.

Not just someone. Nicholas! What on earth was he doing out there in the pouring rain?

He began to head back to the house. Without thinking, Cathryn dashed downstairs to meet him, forgetting that she was still wearing just her night-shirt. She held the door open for him as he limped up the path, and almost dragged him inside.

'Are you crazy?' she demanded. 'Look at you! You're soaked. And you've only been out of hospital for a few days! Are you trying to get pneumonia?'

'No,' replied Nicholas in a very practical tone of voice. 'I've been trying to raise the yellow flag, to let people on the mainland know that we need picking up. And I finally managed it.'

'You're mad,' Cathryn said flatly. 'Getting drenched to the skin just for the sake of some stupid flag.'

'*You're* the one who wants to get off this island,' Nicholas reminded her. 'I'd be quite happy to stay here for a few more days.'

'Are you saying that you did it for me?' she said hotly. 'And I suppose I'll get all the blame when you get whipped back into hospital with some fever! Oh, look at you,' she half groaned. 'You're already shivering. Get those wet clothes off and move nearer the fire.'

Nicholas must have lit the fire before he went out

because the logs were blazing brightly. He pulled off his sopping-wet jumper, and then raised one eyebrow as Cathryn began to drag open the buttons of his shirt.

She caught his gaze and flushed brightly. 'Er—you finish this,' she said very hurriedly. 'I'll—I'll fetch some towels.'

By the time she came back Nicholas had stripped down to his underpants, which made her colour even more vividly.

'If I'd known you were going to get this confused, I'd have undressed in the bathroom,' he said with some amusement.

'I'm not confused! I'm just——'

'Just what?' he questioned her with some interest, the tone of his voice suddenly beginning to change.

'Nothing,' she muttered. She tossed the towels over to him. 'Here, use these.'

He wound one round his waist, and used the other to roughly towel-dry his hair. And all the time he kept looking at her in a way that made her want to turn tail and run. Only she didn't. Something seemed to keep her rooted to the spot.

Nicholas finished towelling his hair, and ran his fingers through it to smooth down its ruffled darkness. Cathryn watched him with uneasy fascination. What was it about this man that had so begun to interest her?

His green gaze was still locked on to her, and there was a new darkness in it now. Then it altered again, catching fire this time, so that the colour of his eyes blazed out amid the gloom of the day.

Cathryn tried to swallow, but suddenly her throat wouldn't work. Hazy presentiments of danger began to form inside her head as a lot of loose ends began to drift together, to form a pattern. And the pattern was one that she definitely didn't want to see.

Just two nights ago, she had recognised how devastating it would be to fall in love with a man like this.

But what if it had already happened?

It couldn't have! she told herself in a panic. There hadn't been time. Anyway, she would have known—would have stopped it.

Stopped it? mocked a small voice inside her head. How?

She didn't know. She was beginning to feel as if she didn't know anything any more. Perhaps that was why she didn't move when Nicholas took two limping but swift steps over to her.

'It's a funny sort of morning, isn't it?' he said in a husky voice. 'In fact, it's been a funny couple of days. And right now, although I know perfectly well that I shouldn't, all I seem to want to do is kiss you. Then keep on kissing you until you're ready to do just about whatever I ask. And I'm beginning to want a great deal,' he went on in an increasingly thick tone.

'I don't think——' Cathryn somehow got out.

'I don't *care* what you think,' he said a little roughly. 'Do you understand that? At this particular moment, I simply don't *care*.

Cathryn understood only too well. An unexpected recklessness filled her own veins. She couldn't remember ever feeling like this before. It scared her half to death and yet somehow exhilarated her.

Not that she had too much time to think about it. Nicholas was already bending his head and taking

the kiss that he wanted. Except that he couldn't stop
at one kiss. His mouth burned on hers, over and
over, as if she were some kind of drug that he had
just discovered and couldn't leave alone.

Her hands touched him, tentatively at first, and
then a little more frantically. She could feel his
muscles tensing under his still damp skin; she heard
the breath catch again, and then again, in his throat.

His mouth slid down the side of her throat, and
where once before it had lightly scorched her, now it
branded her. He seemed to be leaving the stamp of
his possessiveness all over her.

Possessiveness? she wondered dazedly. But she
had the feeling that Nicholas was never possessive
about anything—or anyone.

There was no more chance to wonder about it. He
scooped her up and, despite his injuries, seemed to
lift her easily on to the sofa. He was breathing more
heavily, but she had the feeling that it wasn't from
the few brief moments of exertion.

Nicholas stretched himself out beside her and his
eyes glistened brightly. 'Just like the other night,' he
murmured. 'Only not *quite* the same, Cathryn.'

It always seemed to do something to her when he
spoke her name, and this was no exception. It made
her more vulnerable to him and he seemed to know
it, because he said it again. 'Cathryn.' The syllables
slipped silkily off his tongue and a new warmth
glowed inside her.

The small buttons on her nightshirt were the only
obstacles in his way now, and he disposed of them
with ease. She couldn't tell him to stop because he
was already kissing her again, the subtle movements

of his tongue somehow co-ordinating with the movements of his fingers as they slid down over the warm swell of her breast. Disturbing sensations fluttered inside her, fanned into life by the warmth of him, the scent of him, his gathering closeness as he restlessly moved against her.

This was a very different Nicholas from the bad-tempered man she had known at Sir Charles's flat; or the more relaxed and sometimes even good-humoured person she had come to know since they had been on the island. This man was like a chameleon, she thought a little despairingly. And this was his most dangerous guise of all!

She didn't know what had brought on this abrupt change of mood, but she did know where he was very single-mindedly heading. Nor could she seem to do anything about it. When she rather half-heartedly pushed his hands away from one part of her, they instantly moved on to another, even more rawly sensitive curve of her flesh. He seemed only too aware that she didn't really want him to stop. His tongue tickled and teased, and his fingers slid relentlessly into soft, warm, intimate places, arousing vivid sensations that made her shiver deeply.

Then Nicholas lifted his head for an instant. 'Touch me,' he ordered huskily.

Cathryn didn't even consider disobeying his urgent instruction. His body was hot and hard, his skin damp and supple under her own searching fingertips. She traced out the patterns of scars new and old, and he kissed away her dismay at finding just how many of them there were.

Then he returned his attention to her breasts, lingering over their swollen fullness until she really thought she couldn't stand the exquisite bursts of pleasure for one moment longer.

Nicholas raised his head again and she could see the deep flare of colour along his cheekbones, the wild glitter in his eyes and the taut line of his mouth. His body was tense and hard against hers, with small shivers running through him, forerunners of a much greater pleasure. She half closed her eyes in a dazed, sensual anticipation of what was about to happen. She was beyond thinking about it, or wondering at it. She just knew that it seemed *right*. She was still amazed that the cool, unresponsive Cathryn could want this man so much, but that was all part of the mystery. And perhaps afterwards she would understand it a little better. . .

Nothing happened, though, and Cathryn very slowly opened her eyes again. She found Nicholas was staring down at her with a blaze of deep frustration on his face, and she gazed back at him uneasily.

'What is it?' she whispered.

'Do you know how gorgeous and desirable you look right now?' he said abruptly. Then he rather shakily ran his fingers through his hair. 'For a moment there, I thought I wasn't going to be able to stop. That's never happened to me before. I've always been good at self-control. *Too* damned good, perhaps.'

'Why——?' Her voice came out so croaky that she had to try again. 'Why do you have to stop?'

'Because I can't do this,' Nicholas said roughly. 'You're looking up at me so trustingly, so lovingly, and it's making me feel like a complete bastard because I'm offering you nothing in return. *Nothing*.'

He moved away from her and sat on the edge of the sofa, his head bent against his locked hands so that she couldn't see his face.

Cathryn didn't know what to say to him. There were a lot of words inside her, but they seemed to be stuck in her throat. She just couldn't get them out. In the end, she somehow managed to stand up on her shaking legs.

'Perhaps I'd better go and get dressed,' she said in a voice that came out with amazing steadiness.

'Yes, I think you'd better,' Nicholas agreed, still not looking at her.

Cathryn walked over to the doorway. Then she turned round and looked at him. 'I think that you *were* offering me something,' she said quietly. 'It's just that you couldn't see it.' Then she went up to her room, where she sat on the edge of the bed for a very long time, staring rather blindly into the distance.

What was happening to her? How had she got into this situation? And what did she want from Nicholas Ellis?

Far more than he would ever be prepared to give her, she acknowledged to herself wearily. That was the real problem. It would still have been a problem even if he *hadn't* stopped himself from actually making love to her.

And she was ready to admit that she hadn't wanted him to stop. Cathryn was always painfully honest, even with herself. She wanted to know this man so much better. He wouldn't let her get through to him, though. He was so self-contained, so fiercely independent. He didn't intend to let himself ever love or need someone.

When she at last found the nerve to go downstairs again, she found that Nicholas was fully dressed and sitting by the window. He looked up at her as she came in, and then lifted his dark eyebrows in a gesture of unexpected regret.

'I suppose this is where I apologise for what happened.'

'There's absolutely no need for that,' Cathryn replied levelly.

'Isn't there?' For a moment, his gaze caught and held hers. Unexpectedly, he was the one who then looked away, as if he found the contact between them uncomfortable.

Cathryn looked at him sadly. Could she really have fallen in love with a man who didn't *want* to be loved?

It was beginning to look as if the answer was yes. Idiot! she lectured herself a little despairingly. Why choose someone like Nicholas Ellis? Someone you knew you could never have?

She sighed. She supposed that few people actually chose to fall in love. It just happened, like the proverbial bolt from the blue. And she definitely felt as if she had been hit by something! She couldn't remember ever being so shaky, so uncertain, so downright disturbed.

Nicholas was gazing out of the window again. Cathryn thought at first that he wanted to avoid looking at her. Then she realised he was looking at the sea. 'There's a boat coming in this direction,' he said a few moments later. 'Someone must have seen the yellow flag.'

'You mean, we're finally going to get off the island?'

'It looks like it. You'd better start to get your things together. Then we can leave straight away.'

'Just like that?' She hadn't meant to say any such thing, but the words just slipped out.

Nicholas finally turned to face her. 'It's what you want, isn't it?' he challenged her bluntly.

And Cathryn didn't have the courage to blurt out that she wasn't sure what she wanted any more, that part of her stupidly longed to be marooned here with him for a couple more days.

'Yes, it's what I want,' she said at last, in a flat voice. What was the point in telling him the truth? He obviously didn't want to hear it.

In what seemed to Cathryn like a remarkably short time, she was sitting in the boat of one of the local fishermen, and heading back to the mainland. She and Nicholas hadn't exchanged another word. She watched the island slowly retreating into the distance, and knew that, although she hadn't enjoyed her stay there, she was almost sorry to leave it. And she felt as if she might like to come back again one day. Of course, she never would, she reminded herself quickly. Nicholas was hardly likely to issue an open invitation!

Sir Charles's car was standing just where they had left it. While Nicholas put their luggage in the back, Cathryn slid behind the wheel.

She realised that she didn't feel at all like the same person who had driven down from London just a couple of days ago. She only hoped she could get back to some semblance of normality once she was back among familiar surroundings.

Nicholas got in beside her. 'Let's go,' he said briefly.

Cathryn switched on the ignition, revved up the powerful engine a couple of times, and then headed the car in the direction of home.

It had stopped raining, but the sky was still overcast. A heavy gloom seemed to hang over the countryside, which precisely matched her mood. Nicholas didn't seem inclined to talk, and when she risked a quick glance at him she discovered that he was frowning.

After they had been on the road for a couple of hours, she decided it was time to break the silence.

'Do you want to stop for something to eat?' she asked.

'I'm not hungry. Not for food,' he said rather abruptly.

Cathryn wasn't sure what to make of his answer, and so she decided to ignore it. 'I hope your brother isn't too worried about us. He asked me to leave a phone number where he could get in touch with us. I didn't know then that we were going to end up on an island with no phone.'

'Charles might worry about you,' Nicholas replied tersely. 'He certainly won't worry about me.'

'That's not true!' Cathryn shot back at once. 'If he wasn't worried about you, he'd simply have left you in that hospital.'

'He did what he did out of a sense of responsibility,' Nicholas growled. 'Nothing more.'

Cathryn shook her head. 'I think the pair of you want your heads knocked together! You've only got each other, and yet you've kept up this ridiculous feud all this time.'

'Charles certainly doesn't regard it as ridiculous.'

'That's because he believes you had an affair with his wife,' Cathryn retorted.

Nicholas shot a sideways look at her. 'Perhaps I did,' he suggested.

'You told me that you didn't.'

'And you believed me?'

'Yes,' Cathryn said without hesitation.

'How can you be so sure that I was telling the truth?'

'I just am.' She was aware that he was still looking at her, and she kept her own attention glued to the road.

'You really think that you know me that well?' he asked curiously.

'I know that you wouldn't lie about a thing like that.' When he didn't say anything more, Cathryn gathered up her courage. 'Are you going to tell me what really *did* happen?' she asked.

Nicholas shrugged. 'Since I've told you this much, I might as well tell you the rest. Although I don't know why the hell I'm talking to you about it. I've never said a word about it to anyone before.' He paused for quite a long while, then he went on, 'Helena made quite a few visits to my London flat. Charles eventually found out about the visits, and assumed they were because we'd had an affair.'

'But you hadn't,' Cathryn said with some certainty.

'No, we hadn't,' Nicholas agreed. 'The reason Helena came to see me was because she wanted to borrow some money. A *lot* of money.'

'Money?' echoed Cathryn in a puzzled voice. 'But what for? Surely your brother gave her a generous allowance?'

'Yes, he did. But it wasn't enough. She needed a

lot more,' Nicholas said a little grimly. 'But she wouldn't ask Charles.'

'What did she want all that money for?'

'Remember I told you once that Helena had quite a few weaknesses? Well, one of them was gambling. In fact, it was her *chief* weakness. She lost vast sums, but she still couldn't stop. And she never told Charles. He thought that she just enjoyed the occasional flutter. He had no idea that she had become so addicted to it, or that she had run up enormous gambling debts. Then the people she owed money to started to become nasty. Helena was frightened—in fact, panic-stricken. She didn't know what to do, and so she came running to me for help.'

'Why on earth didn't she just tell your brother?' asked Cathryn. 'If he loved her as much as you say he did, he'd have understood.'

'He might have understood, but Helena was terrified that it would shatter the idealised picture he had of her. She could see their perfect marriage crumbling, and she couldn't stand the thought of that. She made me promise that I would never tell Charles anything about it.'

'And she asked *you* for the money,' Cathryn said slowly. Comprehension slowly dawned inside her head. 'And you gave her your inheritance! That's where all your money went, isn't it? You said it had gone on gambling debts—but they were Helena's debts, not yours!'

Nicholas lifted his shoulders in a gesture of resignation. 'What else could I do? Helena didn't have anyone else to help her, and she was in such a state that I was frightened of what she might do if I turned her away.'

'But after Helena died in the car crash, why didn't you tell your brother about all this?' Cathryn demanded. 'You could so easily have put things right between you.'

'A promise was a promise, even though Helena was dead. Anyway, by then Charles had already convinced himself that we'd had an affair. After Helena's death, a "friend" had told him about Helena's visits to my flat, and he immediately drew his own conclusions. Charles was always obsessively jealous where Helena was concerned. He saw every other man as a threat. I knew there was nothing I could say that would make Charles believe any differently.'

Cathryn was at last beginning to understand how difficult it would be for the two brothers ever to put things right between them. 'You're sure that your brother wouldn't believe your version of events?' she said slowly, at last.

Nicholas shook his head. 'He wouldn't even listen to me if I tried to talk to him about it.'

She gave a deep sigh. 'It seems such a pity that you can't somehow sort this out.'

'We can't,' Nicholas said bluntly. 'Leave it at that. I can live with it.'

Cathryn couldn't help thinking about it during the rest of the drive back to London, though. So many misunderstandings, and both men too proud even to try and sort them out.

They finally drew up outside Sir Charles's flat, but Cathryn didn't immediately get out of the car. Her own problems were beginning to crowd in on her again now.

'You don't need a nursemaid any more,' she said

quietly, turning to Nicholas. 'In fact, I don't think that you ever needed one. I'll come in and collect the rest of my things. Then I think it would be best if I went back to my own flat.'

'You're certain that's what you want to do?'

Cathryn was suddenly angry at his attitude. 'It's what *you* want me to do, isn't it?' she challenged him. When he didn't answer, she got out of the car and ran up the steps to the front door.

It took her a couple of seconds to get the key in the lock because her fingers were shaking. She finally managed it, and went into the silent, empty flat. She decided to go straight to her room, pack her few remaining things, and then clear out straight away. There didn't seem to be any point in prolonging this misery any longer.

Nicholas had already followed her in, though. He came limping over, his face looking unexpectedly grim, and caught hold of her shoulders.

'I think we need to talk about this——' he began.

'I don't want to talk about it!' Cathryn said stubbornly. 'I just want to get out of here.'

His fingers bit deeper into her shoulders. 'You're not going anywhere, not yet. I want——'

'I don't care what you want!' she interrupted him, the turmoil inside her suddenly exploding out in a rush of pure temper. 'And let go of me! You're *hurting* me.'

He didn't seem to realise that she hadn't meant he was hurting her physically. His fingers were already slackening their grip, but before he could release her completely the door to the drawing-room flew open and Cathryn was astonished to see Sir Charles come charging straight at them.

'Get your hands off her, you bastard!' he bawled at his brother bitterly. 'Haven't you hurt enough women in your life?'

Nicholas looked stunned, and his hands renewed their grip on Cathryn's shoulders, as if he suddenly needed her support. Sir Charles wrenched them away, though. Then he spun his brother round to face him.

'I told you to let go of her!' he roared. Then he hit his brother hard on the jaw, sending Nicholas crashing to the ground.

CHAPTER NINE

CATHRYN couldn't believe this was happening. Sir Charles had already raised his fist, as if he was ready to hit his brother again as soon as he tried to get up. Nicholas took a very long time hauling himself to his feet, though, and seemed to be making no effort to defend himself.

'Get up and fight, you damned coward!' Sir Charles taunted him.

'I won't raise my hand against you,' Nicholas replied quietly.

Cathryn couldn't stand it any more. 'Stop this!' she cried. 'Just *stop* it. I won't have anyone fighting over me!'

'But this isn't about you, Cathryn,' said Nicholas. Then his gaze swivelled searchingly to his brother's face. 'Or is it?' he questioned softly. 'Do *you* want Cathryn, Charles?'

Sir Charles instantly looked shocked. 'Of course not! Cathryn works for me, that's all. There's certainly nothing else between us, if that's what you're insinuating. But I won't see her manhandled by anyone. And certainly not by you!'

Surprisingly, Nicholas seemed to relax after he had heard his brother confirm that he had no romantic interest in Cathryn. He rubbed his jaw ruefully, and then glanced up at Charles.

'Why don't you ask Cathryn if she minds being manhandled by me?' he asked drily.

'I'll ask her no such thing,' Sir Charles shot back angrily. 'Cathryn's already been through quite enough at your hands.'

'Cathryn's been through *nothing* at my hands,' Nicholas retorted sharply. Then he briefly checked himself. 'At least, nothing that went too far,' he finally amended. 'If you don't believe me, just ask her yourself.'

'She's probably too intimidated by you to give me a truthful answer——' Sir Charles said fiercely.

'I'm not intimidated by Nicholas,' Cathryn cut in quietly. 'He's never hurt me—not physically—and he's never forced me into anything. He'd never do that to anyone.'

'Ha!' came Sir Charles's disbelieving response. 'You just don't know him very well.'

'She thinks she does,' Nicholas said in a voice that suddenly sounded very tired.

'Then she doesn't know much about your past, does she?' Sir Charles responded bitterly.

'I know that you think he had an affair with your wife,' Cathryn said in a very clear voice, not quite sure how she had found the courage to say such a thing to Sir Charles. 'But he didn't.'

Sir Charles's face went absolutely white, and a warning darkness spread over Nicholas's features. 'Cathryn, don't!' he instructed curtly. 'Stay out of this.'

'How can I stay out of it? The two of you have dragged me right into the middle of it!' She turned round to face Sir Charles. 'Your wife *did* visit Nicholas's flat, but not for the reasons you thought. She wanted to borrow money from him, that was all.'

'If she had needed money, she would have come

to me,' Sir Charles said flatly. 'I always let her have whatever she wanted.'

'She wanted a *lot* of money. She had run up huge gambling debts, but she was frightened to tell you about them.'

Sheer disbelief showed on Sir Charles's face. 'I know she liked to gamble now and then, but—huge debts? And how could she possibly have been frightened of me? I loved her! She knew how much I loved her.'

'You put her on a pedestal,' Cathryn said in a quieter voice. 'She was scared to death that you'd love her a lot less—or not at all—if she ever fell off that pedestal.'

'So, perhaps Helena needed money,' Sir Charles conceded in a harsh voice. He swung round to look at his brother in disgust. 'But why would she go to *Nicholas* unless there was something between them?'

Nicholas looked resigned. 'I told you this would happen,' he said, turning to Cathryn. 'All you're doing is making things worse.'

'How can things possibly get any worse?' she demanded. She turned back to Sir Charles. 'Why are you so sure that your brother had an affair with your wife?'

'I know him,' growled Sir Charles. 'I know his track record with women. And anyway, Helena changed. Those last few months, she was—different towards me,' he muttered, obviously finding it hard to get the words out.

'Of course she was different,' Nicholas said evenly. 'She was being hounded by some very unpleasant people. She was scared to death. No one in that sort of situation behaves normally.'

For the first time, a shadow of doubt showed on Sir Charles's face. Then it was followed by a grimace of pure pain.

'If she was in so much trouble, why didn't she come to *me*?' he said with some bitterness. 'Why couldn't she even talk to me about it?'

'Because she loved you too much,' Nicholas replied. 'She was deeply ashamed of her addiction to gambling. On top of that, she was terrifed you'd despise her if you ever found out about it. She went to quite desperate lengths to keep it from you.'

Sir Charles was silent for a very long time, as if he was trying to take in everything that had been said; then his shoulders slowly began to slump. His aggressiveness melted away and he suddenly looked a dozen years older. He turned to Nicholas and Cathryn, as if he was about to say something. Instead, though, he turned round and abruptly walked out of the room.

'Let him go,' said Nicholas, when Cathryn started to go after him. 'He needs to be on his own for a while.' His dark brows drew together. 'Finding out that Helena couldn't confide in him, that she had to go to someone else when she was in trouble—that's hurt him just as badly as thinking she had an affair.'

'I suppose I shouldn't have said anything,' said Cathryn unhappily.

'No, you shouldn't,' Nicholas agreed rather curtly. 'I can live with my brother's animosity, but I'm not sure that Charles can live with the knowledge that his wife wouldn't come to him for help when she was in trouble.'

There was a long, tense silence between the two of

them, which was only broken when Sir Charles unexpectedly walked back into the room.

'I need time to think this over,' he said abruptly. 'I think it would be best if I went back to America for a while. I only came back because I had a short break in my schedule, and I was worried about you, Cathryn. You'd gone off with Nicholas, I didn't even know where, and—and I didn't trust my brother,' he said in a low voice.

'Do you trust him now?' asked Cathryn quietly.

Sir Charles looked uncharacteristically indecisive. 'I don't know,' he muttered at last. Then he looked at Cathryn. 'What are *you* going to do now?' he asked her.

'I think Cathryn needs a break—from both of us,' Nicholas cut in, answering for her. 'Give her a few days off, Charles.'

'I don't need time off,' Cathryn said quickly. 'I can be back at work in the morning.'

'I don't want to see you in the office before next week,' Sir Charles instructed. 'And if you don't want to come back at all—if you want to use the time to find another job—I'll quite understand. We've mixed you up in our family problems, Cathryn, and you don't look as if you've enjoyed it very much. You might decide that you want to get right away from both of us.'

But Cathryn understood only too well by now that she didn't want to get away from Nicholas—not ever. Unfortunately, he very much seemed to want to get away from *her*. No ties, no commitments—that was how he ran his life, and he obviously didn't intend to make any changes.

'I've rung for a taxi to take me to the airport,' went on Sir Charles. 'Would you like a lift somewhere?'

'Back to my flat, please,' said Cathryn in a small voice. 'If it's not too much trouble.'

She glanced at Nicholas, a small part of her still hoping that he would tell her he didn't want her to go. He remained silent, though, sitting in a chair now and looking rather withdrawn. Cathryn had the impression that he wanted both of them just to go and leave him on his own.

The two brothers didn't say a word to each other until the taxi pulled up outside. Then Sir Charles looked at Nicholas.

'You'll stay here until I get back from America?'

'If that's what you want,' replied Nicholas in a rather flat voice.

'You'll be all right on your own?'

'Of course.'

And he was telling the truth about that, Cathryn thought miserably. Nicholas would always be all right on his own. *She* was the one who was going to find it incredibly hard to get back to her normal existence.

She climbed into the taxi beside Sir Charles, and realised that Nicholas hadn't even said goodbye to her. She blinked rather hard, and fiercely told herself that it didn't matter. She wasn't going to let it get to her.

'I think I ought to apologise to you,' said Sir Charles, his voice breaking through the cloud of depression that was settling over her. 'I never meant you to get so caught up in our family problems.'

'I'm the one who ought to be apologising,' she said

in a low tone. 'I shouldn't have interfered, and said the things that I did.'

'About my wife?' Sir Charles gave a faintly twisted smile. 'Perhaps I needed to hear them. It's been a long time since anyone even dared to mention her name to me.' He paused for a moment, then said rather abruptly, 'Do you think that Nicholas tells lies?'

'No, I don't,' she said without hesitation.

He looked at her with unexpected gentleness. 'You don't think that your opinion of my brother might be a little biased?'

'It might be,' she admitted reluctantly. 'But I think he's basically very straightforward. If he'd had an affair with your wife, he'd have quite openly admitted it and then taken the consequences.'

Sir Charles was silent again for some time. 'There were several times when I suspected Helena of having an affair,' he said at last, in a rather harsh voice. 'Looking back, I don't think she ever did. It was all in my mind. Perhaps it would have been better if we'd never met,' he went on with a dark shake of his head. 'I was always so obsessed with her. She couldn't have found that at all easy to live with. She couldn't even come to me when she was in such serious trouble.'

'Sometimes it's easier to talk to someone you're not emotionally involved with,' Cathryn tried to console him.

'Nicholas——' he growled, with another shake of his head '—she went to Nicholas.'

'Only for money,' Cathryn said with absolute certainty.

Sir Charles looked as if he very much wanted to

believe that. 'I remember lecturing Nicholas on the way he squandered his inheritance,' he said heavily. 'But he didn't squander it, did he? He gave it to my wife.' He looked at Cathryn. 'If I tried to give that money back to him, do you think he'd accept it?'

She gave a rueful smile. 'I shouldn't think so. He's got his own peculiar standards.'

Sir Charles studied her thoughtfully. 'You *have* got to know my brother well, haven't you?'

Luckily, the taxi pulled up outside her flat at that point, which saved her from having to answer. She rather quickly scrambled out, hoping Sir Charles would say no more on the subject of Nicholas. She really didn't think she could take it right now.

He merely smiled at her, though. 'Let me know if you still want to work for me, after you've taken a few days' break,' he instructed her. 'I hope you will— the office will be in chaos without you!'

The taxi pulled away then, heading in the direction of the airport, leaving Cathryn to trudge tiredly into her one-roomed flat. Once, she had thought it cosy. Now, after the spacious luxury of Sir Charles's apartment, it merely looked cramped.

She flung her luggage down in the corner, and then flopped in a depressed heap on the bed. She had the feeling that the next few days weren't going to be any fun at all.

Cathryn soon found herself wishing that she could go back to work. That would have been much better than sitting around all day, with far too much time on her hands to think about things that she didn't *want* to think about. Sir Charles had ordered her to take a break, though, and she didn't have much choice except to obey. Anyway, she wasn't sure it would be a good idea to go back. Perhaps she should try and find another job. While she worked for Sir Charles, there was always a chance that she might run into Nicholas again one day.

Nicholas—even now she didn't understand how he had so thoroughly managed to insinuate himself into her life. Just a few days with him, and wham! She was in broken little pieces that wouldn't fit back together again.

Rather half-heartedly, she scoured the 'situations vacant' columns, looking for a job that promised to be as interesting as the one she already had. She didn't find any, though—perhaps because she wasn't looking very hard. By the end of the week, she wasn't eating properly, was sleeping hardly at all, and all because of someone that she couldn't put out of her head. Yet she knew she had to do it. Nicholas liked short-term affairs, nothing too serious. No matter how she felt about him, she couldn't offer him that. Cathryn knew she wouldn't be able to handle it when it was over. The way she felt now would be nothing compared to the devastation that would sweep over her when Nicholas walked away.

She lost weight; she looked and felt lousy. If this was love, she didn't think much of it. By the weekend, feeling desperate, she phoned her parents and asked if she could go home for a couple of days. As always, they welcomed her with open arms. Her mother fussed over her, and her father hinted heavily that they would love to have her home permanently. Cathryn felt the old wrench at her heart. She loved them both, but she just couldn't live with them. She wasn't their little girl any longer, but they didn't seem able to treat her like an adult. In the end, the old sense of suffocation began to close in on her again, and she knew she had to get back to London. She told them she had to be at work the following morning, and they reluctantly accepted her decision.

In fact, Cathryn was still in two minds about whether to return to her present job or not. Sir Charles would be back from America by now, though, and expecting to see her. Either way, she had to see him and let him know her decision.

She dressed carefully, but couldn't do much about her lacklustre appearance—or the lack of sparkle in her eyes. When she reached the office, she realised that she still hadn't made a decision. Perhaps she could talk it over with Sir Charles. He had already guessed that she had managed to get herself emotionally tied up in knots with his brother. He might be able to help her make up her mind.

Her own desk was piled up with work that had accumulated during her absence. Firmly ignoring it, she walked towards Sir Charles's office and knocked lightly on his door.

A voice ordered her to come in. She took a deep breath, opened the door, and marched in. Then she stopped dead.

Nicholas was sitting behind Sir Charles's desk.

Cathryn simply stood and gaped at him. She knew she couldn't have gone any paler if she had seen a ghost. It was just so totally unexpected, seeing him sitting there. She felt as if someone had punched the stuffing out of her and forgotten to put it back again.

'Do you want to sit down?' offered Nicholas calmly. 'You look as if your legs are about to give way.'

'N-no,' she managed to splutter shakily. 'I'm—I'm all right.'

'You don't look all right,' he remarked. 'It's actually quite a boost to my ego, having this sort of effect on a woman.'

'I'm sure it's happened before,' she shot back, her voice more tart now as she began to recover from the shock of seeing him.

Nicholas got slowly to his feet. His stick was propped up against the chair. He didn't use it, though. Instead, he took a couple of steps forward and then perched himself on the edge of the desk.

'Not as often as you think,' he said with clear amusement. He studied her face. 'Don't you have any questions you want to ask me?' he prompted gently. 'Such as, what am I doing here? Where's my brother?'

Cathryn decided that she didn't want to know what he was doing here—not yet. Instead, she stuck to his second question, which seemed a lot safer.

'Where is Sir Charles?'

'Back at the flat,' replied Nicholas. 'He returned from America last Friday. We've just spent the weekend together.'

Cathryn's eyebrows shot up. 'Peacefully?'

'Relatively peacefully,' replied Nicholas drily. 'Things aren't perfect between us yet. The situation's been bad for too long—it's too much to hope for an overnight miracle. He's finally beginning to accept that I never laid a finger on Helena, though.'

'How did you convince him of that?'

'I didn't. *You* did,' said Nicholas simply.

'Me?' she said in disbelief. 'How?'

'Charles trusts your judgement, and, since you

believe my version of events, he's forcing himself to do the same. It isn't easy for him. He was always obsessively jealous where Helena was concerned, and he isn't over it even yet. But he's finally beginning to get the whole thing into some kind of perspective, and realising that he's never been able to be very rational where Helena was concerned.'

'It's funny, isn't it?' mused Cathryn. 'He's such a practical man in most other ways.'

'Not funny at all,' remarked Nicholas. 'When love hits you that hard, rationality flies right out of the window. In fact, *everything* flies out of the window. I thought you were beginning to understand that,' he said gently, his green gaze fixing intently on her.

Cathryn's nerve-ends squirmed. She didn't like the way this conversation was going.

'I still don't know what you're doing here,' she said rather sharply.

'Charles thought it would be a good idea if we met on neutral ground.'

Her eyes grew wary. 'Why do we need to meet at all?'

'If I knew the answer to that question, I wouldn't be in such a very confused state myself,' he answered wryly.

'You? Confused?' she echoed in sheer disbelief.

A faint smile touched Nicholas's mouth. 'Unbelievable, isn't it?' he agreed gravely. 'But, you see, I've been having a few problems these last few days.'

Worry instantly showed on her face. 'Medical problems?'

'Not exactly. Although I've been getting some very physical symptoms.'

'What kind of symptoms?'

'Remember the morning I got soaking wet, and stripped off? And we both very nearly got carried away?' he prompted.

Cathryn immediately flushed. She remembered only too well!

'I was very noble that morning. Pulled back just in time, and promised myself that that was the last time I'd lay my hands on you like that. Only I've been regretting it ever since,' he went on, to her amazement. 'I've been waking up in the middle of the night wanting you so much that I'd have sold my soul to have you there beside me. I thought it would get better after a couple of days, that it was only to be expected after all those celibate months in hospital. It's got worse, though. And the really strange thing is that I don't want just any woman. It's got to be you.' His gaze held hers thoughtfully. 'Why do you suppose that is, Cathryn?'

'I don't know,' she got out in a choked voice.

'Nor did I, for quite a while. Then Charles found me prowling around the flat in the middle of the night, like the proverbial cat on hot bricks. He got the whole story out of me, and promptly put me right on a few things.'

Cathryn's head was beginning to spin slightly. 'What sort of things?' she asked rather hoarsely.

'Such as the fact that I can't keep using my job as an excuse for not having the guts to take on a serious relationship. And that there *are* women who can cope with the long absences and the stresses caused by a job like mine.' Nicholas's green eyes rested on her placidly. 'Charles seems to think that you'd cope with them very well indeed.'

'What makes him think that I'd want to cope?' she said warily.

'Charles knows a great deal about the symptoms of love. He's had a lot of first-hand experience, so he easily recognises it in other people. He reckons that we're both suffering from it.'

'*Both*?' Cathryn croaked.

'I reacted in much the same way,' Nicholas admitted cheerfully. Then his eyes gleamed. 'You still look very pale. Are you sure you don't want to sit down?'

Cathryn decided that she would take up his offer this time. She couldn't remember when her legs had last felt this weak!

'How—I mean, what—well, what are we going to do about it?' she somehow managed to get out at last.

'There only seem to be two alternatives,' Nicholas remarked. 'We can forget about the whole thing— difficult,' he commented drily, 'but probably a lot more comfortable in the long run. Or we can work out where we want to go from here.'

Cathryn couldn't quite believe he was saying these things to her. 'Where do *you* want to go?' she asked unsteadily.

Nicholas gave a wolfish grin. 'You want a truthful answer? Straight to bed! But although that would be extremely pleasant in the short term, it wouldn't really solve any of our problems. This is only going to work if we're prepared to make some compromises.'

'What sort of compromises?'

'For a start, I'm returning to work at the end of the month.'

'Are you well enough?' she asked worriedly.

'I will be by then. Another few days, and I won't need this stick any more. A couple more weeks, and I should be moving around almost normally. You'll find that out, if you decide to stick around,' he added, with a totally wicked grin.

Cathryn swallowed hard. She found she liked the idea of Nicholas being completely mobile.

'There is one small snag, though,' he went on. 'They're posting me to the Far East. I'll be there for several months, maybe even longer.' Before Cathryn had a chance to look thoroughly downcast at this piece of news, he added, 'I want to take you with me. You'd have to give up your job with my brother, though. How do you feel about it?'

'I'd like to come with you,' she said without a moment's hesitation.

Nicholas immediately looked extremely pleased. 'There's one other thing,' he added. 'It would be a lot easier all round if we were married.'

'Married?' she yelped, fresh waves of shock rushing right through her.

'Don't you like the idea?'

'I like it a lot! But I thought you were the original confirmed bachelor.'

'So did I,' Nicholas said ruefully. 'Which just goes to show how one particular female can change your view of things. And Charles insists that I make an honest woman of you. He's very protective towards you—takes his duties as your future brother-in-law very seriously. I don't think he'll let me near you again unless I do this right.'

Cathryn stiffened. 'I don't want you to be forced into anything. I'd rather leave things as they are.'

'Well, I wouldn't,' Nicholas replied calmly. 'I'm

quite looking forward to the whole thing.' His gaze suddenly glittered. 'It'll be a whole new experience—for both of us.'

She gulped again. 'Where—where would we live?' she asked shakily. 'When we're not tramping round the world, that is.'

'There's my flat in London. Or we could find somewhere else, if you'd rather. And there's always the island if we want to get away from everything,' he reminded her, with a slow smile.

The island—Cathryn found, to her surprise, that her memories of it had softened considerably.

'I suppose it would be a lot more pleasant in the summer,' she conceded. 'And it would be a great place to take kids.'

'Kids?' repeated Nicholas in a startled voice, as if that thought had only just occurred to him. 'Kids,' he said again in a more thoughtful tone, as if slowly getting used to the idea—and even liking it.

'My parents would want a big wedding,' she warned him. 'I'm an only child, remember. This is the one chance they'll get to put on an impressive display.'

'How impressive?' Nicholas asked warily.

'Very! Bridesmaids, banks of flowers, bells ringing, huge cake, loads of guests—can you face it?'

'I suppose I'll have to,' he said with resignation.

Cathryn shook her head in disbelief. 'You're really willing to go through all that?'

'It looks like it.'

At last, she began to relax, and the shadow of a smile spread over her face. 'I'm finally beginning to believe that you really do love me—even though you've never actually said it!'

Nicholas immediately looked discomfited. 'I'm not very good at saying things like that. You'd better get used to not hearing it very often.'

'Just once would be nice,' she gently pushed him.

'Well—I—I love you,' he got out with some difficulty.

'It'll get easier with practice,' she told him cheerfully.

'I certainly hope so! By the way, if your parents are going to insist on this big wedding, they'd better make a start on organising it. I want us to get married before we leave for the Far East. That gives us just under four weeks.'

'Don't worry. My mother can move mountains when she puts her mind to it. I'll give her a ring later today.'

'I suppose I ought to meet them,' reflected Nicholas. 'Perhaps we could drive down at the weekend.' He looked uncharacteristically anxious. 'Do you suppose they'll like me?'

'I'm afraid they won't actually approve of you,' Cathryn said regretfully. 'They always wanted me to marry a professional man with good prospects. A banker or a solicitor would have been ideal. An accountant or civil servant would have been just about acceptable. I'm afraid a foreign correspondent isn't at all the sort of man they had in mind.'

'I'll charm them into liking me,' Nicholas said more comfortably. Then, when Cathryn looked at him sceptically, he went on, 'You don't think I can be charming?'

'Oh, I'm sure that you can be absolutely anything you want to be. It's just that I haven't actually seen the charming side of you yet!'

'You will,' he assured her. Then he grinned. 'It's probably a great advantage that you've seen so many of my bad points. It'll come as a nice surprise when you discover my good side.'

'I'll look forward to it,' Cathryn said with an answering grin. Then she looked at him curiously. 'When did you discover that you actually—well, that you were. . .'

'In love with you?' Nicholas finished for her, as she floundered slightly. 'It was when my brother hit me on the jaw. For some reason, it seemed to knock some sense into me. I could see you looking down at me with all that concern on your face, and I suddenly thought how nice it was to have someone to care about me so much. And how nice it would be to come home to you every night. I was so staggered by that thought that I stayed down on the floor much longer than I actually had to,' he remarked with a gentle lift of his eyebrows.

'But you let me leave the flat without saying a single word to me,' she reminded him.

'That was because I didn't know what to say! I couldn't suddenly blurt out that I seemed to have been hit by this bolt of lightning. It sounded ridiculous, even to me. Anyway, I thought it was perhaps only a temporary thing, and that I'd get over it.'

'But you didn't?' she said a little anxiously.

'No, I didn't. And it doesn't look as if I'm ever going to.' He ran his fingers a little restlessly through his hair. 'I'm getting very tired of talking,' he said in a more husky voice. 'Why don't you come over here and let me show you just how much you've managed to get to me?'

Cathryn stood up and found that her legs were still

weak. She managed to take the half dozen steps that separated her from Nicholas, though, and gave a small sigh of utter contentment as she felt the already familiar sensation of his arms coming round her.

Nicholas looked down at her. 'You're an amazing girl,' he muttered. 'You've only been in my life a very short time, and yet you've already turned it completely upside-down. What are you going to do to me over the next few years?'

'I'm going to love you,' replied Cathryn softly. 'I think that you need an awful lot of loving.'

'I need *you*,' he confessed. 'And I didn't think I'd ever say that to anyone.'

He shut up after that, and indulged instead in a long kiss that left both of them a little breathless.

When it was over, they moved even closer instead of drawing apart. Cathryn wound her arms around his neck, buried her face in his shoulder, and still found it hard to believe that she wasn't dreaming all of this. She had the feeling that Nicholas was going to convince her over the next few days, though!

His fingers skimmed restlessly up and down her spine, and his mouth burrowed under her hair, finding the warm, soft skin at the base of her throat. He nibbled briefly, and then gave a quiet sigh.

'What is it?' she asked.

'I was just wishing that we weren't in Charles's office,' he said wryly. 'It puts definite limits on what I want to do!'

Since she could feel the hard ache of his body, she knew perfectly well what he wanted from her. He eased her away from him a little, to keep his frustration within limits, and contented himself with another fiercely demanding kiss.

'There are other places we could go,' she said a little shyly.

'I know,' he growled. 'And I'm trying very hard not to give in to the temptation.'

'You are?' She blinked at him in surprise. 'Why?'

'Because I've got to face your parents at the weekend, and I'm not sure I can look them straight in the eye if I've just taken their daughter to bed!'

Cathryn gazed at him in delight. 'Nicholas, you're old-fashioned!'

One dark eyebrow shot up. 'That's the first time I've ever been called that.' His fingers cupped the swell of her breast, lingered for a long, delicious moment over the small, hard peak, and then regretfully withdrew again.

'I'm going to drive myself a little crazy if I keep this up for much longer,' he muttered.

'What should we do instead, then?' she asked, her own voice increasingly breathless.

'First, we'll go and buy a ring. Perhaps your parents will approve of me more quickly if we go along with all the formalities. And afterwards we'll go and see Charles, to tell him that he's about to lose a secretary, but gain a sister-in-law.'

'And then?' Cathryn prompted softly, leaning gently against him.

Nicholas gave a faint groan. 'And then I might have to forget all my good intentions! Perhaps I could wear dark glasses at the weekend. Then I could look at your parents without giving anything away!'

That sounded very satisfactory to Cathryn. She had begun by not wanting to have anything to do with this man. Now she didn't want to let him out of her sight for a single second.

And, amazingly, he felt exactly the same way about her. It was going to take her a very long time to get used to that remarkable fact.

Then Nicholas smiled down at her, his green eyes open and loving, and it occurred to her that it might not take any time at all.

TWO COMPELLING READS FOR MAY 1990

TESS   *Katherine Burton*   £2.99

In the third book of this sensational quartet of sisters, the bestselling author of *Sweet Summer Heat* creates Tess. Tormented by the guilt of her broken marriage and afraid to risk the pain again, Tess is torn by desire. But was Seth Taylor the right choice in helping her to get over the pain of the past?

SPRING THUNDER   *Sandra James*   £2.99

After a traumatic divorce and the unfamiliar demands of a new born son, Jessica is determined to start a new life running a garden centre. Tough, reliable Brody was hired to help, but behind the facade of job hunting is hidden the fact that he was being paid to destroy Jessica…whatever the cost.

W RLDWIDE

Mills & Boon

A Free Mills & Boon Romance for you!

At Mills & Boon we always do our best to ensure that our books are just what you want to read. To do this we need your help! Please spare a few minutes to answer the questions below and overleaf and, as a special thank you, we will send you a FREE Mills & Boon Romance when you return your completed questionnaire.

Don't forget to fill in your name and address so we know where to send your FREE BOOK.

Please tick the appropriate boxes to indicate your answers.

1 (a) **Are you a regular Mills & Boon Romance reader?**

Yes ❏   No ❏

(b) **If you are, how many Romances do you read each month?**

1 ❏   2-4 ❏   4-6 ❏
more than 6 ❏

2 **We'd like your views on which season your Romances are set in:-**

(a) **For example would you mind reading a book set at Christmas in July?**   Yes ❏   No ❏   Don't mind ❏

(b) **Would you prefer to read about hot summery settings in the Summer and winter settings in the Winter?**

Yes ❏   No ❏   Don't mind ❏

3 (a) **Would you like to read about older heroines?**

Yes ❏   No ❏   Don't mind ❏

Please complete overleaf

(b) If yes, from which age group, please tick one to indicate your choice.

in their thirties? ☐   forties? ☐   fifties? ☐

4 Do you like the hero to be older than the heroine?

Yes ☐   No ☐   Don't mind ☐

5 In your view what is the ideal age gap between hero and heroine?

5 years ☐   10 years ☐   20 years ☐   No age gap ☐

6 Is there anything you particularly like or dislike about Mills & Boon books?

_____

_____

7 What is your favourite type of book apart from romantic fiction?

_____

_____

8 What age group are you in?

Under 25 ☐   25-34 ☐
35-54 ☐   55-65 ☐
Over 65 please state_____

9 Are you a Reader Service subscriber?

Yes ☐   No ☐

Thank you for your help. We hope that you enjoy your FREE book.

Post this page TODAY TO: **Mills & Boon Reader Survey FREEPOST, P.O. Box 236, Croydon CR9 9EL.**

Mr/Mrs/Ms/Miss_____   EDQ3

Address_____

_____

_____

_____ Postcode_____

mps MAILING PREFERENCE SERVICE

DREAM SONG TITLES COMPETITION
HOW TO ENTER

Listed below are 5 incomplete song titles. To enter simply choose the missing word from the selection of words listed and write it on the dotted line provided to complete each song title.

A. . . . . .DREAMS   LOVER

B. DAY DREAM . . . . -   ELECTRIC

C. DREAM . . . .   CHRISTMAS

D. UPON A DREAM   BELIEVER

E. I'M DREAMING OF A WHITE . . . .   ONCE

When you have completed each of the song titles, fill in the box below, placing the songs in an order ranging from the one you think is the most romantic, through to the one you think is the least romantic.

Use the letter corresponding to the song titles when filling in the five boxes.

For example: If you think C. is the most romantic song, place the letter C. in the 1st box.

	1st	2nd	3rd	4th	5th
LETTER OF CHOSEN SONG					

MRS/MISS/MR . . . .

ADDRESS . . . .

. . . .

POSTCODE . . . . .COUNTRY . . . .

CLOSING DATE: 31st DECEMBER, 1990

PLEASE SEND YOUR COMPLETED ENTRY TO EITHER:

Dream Book Offer, Eton House, 18-24 Paradise Road, Richmond, Surrey, ENGLAND TW9 1SR.

OR (Readers in Southern Africa)

Dream Book Offer, IBS Pty Ltd., Private Bag X3010, Randburg 2125, SOUTH AFRICA.

Please retain this section.

RULES AND CONDITIONS
FOR THE COMPETITION AND DREAM BOOK OFFER

1. These offers are open to all Mills & Boon readers with the exception of those living in countries where such a promotion is illegal, employees of the Harlequin Group of Companies, their agents, anyone directly connected with this offer and their families. 2. All applications must be received by the closing date, 31st December, 1990. 3. Responsibility cannot be accepted for entries lost, damaged or delayed in transit. Illegible applications will not be accepted. Proof of postage is not proof of receipt. 4. The prize winner of the competition will be notified by post 28 days after the closing date. 5. Only one application per household is permitted for the Competition and Dream Book. 6. The prize for the competition will be awarded to the entrant who, in the opinion of the judges, has given the correct answers to the competition and in the event of a tie a further test of skill and judgement will be used to determine the winner. 7. You may be mailed with other offers as a result of these applications.

 **Mills & Boon**

4 ROMANCES & 2 GIFTS - YOURS
ABSOLUTELY FREE!

An irresistible invitation from Mills & Boon! Please accept our offer of 4 free books, a pair of decorative glass oyster dishes and a special MYSTERY GIFT...Then, if you choose, go on to enjoy 6 more exciting Romances every month for just £1.35 each postage and packing free.

Send the coupon below at once to -
Reader Service, FREEPOST, P.O. Box 236, Croydon, Surrey CR9 9EL

✂ - *No stamp required* - - - - - - - - - - - - - - - -

YES! Please rush me my **4 Free Romances and 2 FREE Gifts !** Please also reserve me a Reader Service Subscription. so I can look forward to receiving 6 Brand New Romances each month, for just £8.10 total. Post and packing is **free**, and there's a free monthly Mills & Boon Newsletter. If I choose not to subscribe I shall write to you within 10 days - I understand I can keep the books and gifts whatever I decide. I can cancel or suspend my subscription at any time, I am over18.

EP60R

NAME _____

ADDRESS _____

_____

_____ **POSTCODE** _____

SIGNATURE _____

The right is reserved to refuse an application and change the terms of this offer. You may be mailed with other offers as a result of this application. Offer expires Dec 31st 1989 and is limited to one per household. offer applies in the UK and Eire only. Overseas send for details